# 'I Know That Some Nights You Dance Alone In Your Kitchen, Megan,'

Nick said, stepping closer. 'That tells me you still have faith in your hopes and dreams. Let me in on them, sweetheart.'

Her hopes and dreams. Megan winced when she remembered the haughty speech she had delivered to Nick a decade ago about her hopes and dreams. How different her life had turned out.

'Nick, you just don't understand.'

'No, I don't,' he said. 'But doesn't it mean something to you that I want to?'

Then he closed his arms around her and rocked her gently in his embrace. Closing her eyes, she quietly acknowledged the truth to herself.

No one had ever held her like this. No one had ever made her feel so safe, yet so close to danger.

And it felt so good she never wanted to let go.

Dear Reader,

Well, if you are off on holiday or staying at home this month, here are the perfect stories for you to relax with and enjoy.

Firstly, meet **Man of the Month** for August, Joe Dana. He ends up nearly delivering a baby in a vegetable garden and somehow, when the crisis is over, finds it impossible to leave. This, the latest from Dixie Browning, *Look What the Stork Brought*, is one of her best yet.

Doreen Owens Malek brings together a rugged rogue and a passionate lonely woman in *Big Sky Drifter*. And in Raye Morgan's *The Hand-Picked Bride* there are sparks flying between Grant Fargo and the woman he'd chosen to be his brother's wife.

*Wife for a Night* by Carol Grace is the sexy tale of a woman who was too young for her handsome fiancé six years ago but has since grown up. Lastly, Susan Crosby and Susan Connell complete this wonderful line-up with tales of men who have marriage on their minds!

There's plenty to look forward to next month when Anne McAllister brings us her **Man of the Month**, Shane Nichols. We also start up two new mini-series: Elizabeth Bevarly brings us three tales about the antics of a matchmaking comet—and Metsy Hingle kicks off **Right Bride, Wrong Groom**—no prizes for guessing what that's about!

Happy reading!

The Editors

# Tall, Dark and Temporary

# SUSAN CONNELL

™SILHOUETTE

Desire®

*Silhouette, Silhouette Desire and Colophon
are registered trademarks of Harlequin Books S.A.,
used under licence.*

*First published in Great Britain 1998
Silhouette Books, Eton House, 18-24 Paradise Road,
Richmond, Surrey TW9 1SR*

© Susan Connell 1998

ISBN 0 373 76120 1

*22-9808*

*Printed and bound in Spain
by Litografía Rosés S.A., Barcelona*

## SUSAN CONNELL

has a love of travelling that has taken her all over the world—Greece, Spain, Portugal, Central and South America, to name just a few places. While working for the foreign service she met a U.S. Navy pilot, and eight days later they were engaged. Twenty-one years and several moves later, Susan, her husband, Jim, and daughter, Catherine, call the New Jersey shore home. When she's not writing, her part-time job at a local bookstore, Mediterranean cooking and travelling with her family are some of her favourite activities.

### Other novels by Susan Connell

*Silhouette Desire®*

†Reese: The Untamed
Rebel's Spirit
How To Succeed at Love

†*Sons and Lovers*

Cindy Gerard and Leanne Banks—

Recently Voted: The Friends Most Likely To
Stay on My Speed-dial

# Prologue

"**H**ey, girlfriend, who says you can't go home again?"

Another warm wave of nostalgia washed over Megan Sloan at the spirited sound of her old high-school classmate. Megan was already smiling as she turned to face the woman walking toward her across the dimly lit dance floor.

"Unlike you, Rebecca, some of us never left," Megan said, sharing a hug. "I'm so glad you made it back."

"Me, too." Rebecca Barnett reached out to run her hand through the curtain of crepe-paper streamers billowing behind them. "It's hard to believe it's been ten years since we graduated from this place."

"Not if you squint a little. Try it. It's like being back at the senior prom."

Megan knew; she'd been stealing filtered looks back to the past since the first couple wandered out onto the dance floor over an hour ago. The silly thrill she experienced each time she did it was embarrassing. Or would have been if anyone knew what memories she was stirring up. But that's what high-school reunions were all about. Reliving moments from another lifetime. At least, the good ones, she thought, glancing toward the red and white streamers.

She fidgeted with one of her earrings, then took a long, quiet breath before turning her attention back to Rebecca. The strikingly attractive brunette tilted her head and dutifully squinted for several seconds before turning a doubtful gaze to Megan.

"I don't know, Meggie," Rebecca said, a teasing reprimand in her tone. "As the person in charge of this reunion, you did one heck of a good job. But that's not exactly Prom Night, Part Two going on out there."

"And what's not working for you?" Megan asked, pretending disbelief. "The fake French café? The golden oldies?"

Rebecca stepped closer. "John Canfield and Freddie Wagner," she whispered behind the curled fingers of one hand.

Leave it to Rebecca to make her feel as if they were standing by their lockers exchanging high-school gossip once again. "What about them?" Megan asked, while somehow managing not to move her lips.

"Their hair," Rebecca whispered. "How could they have lost so much of it in just one decade?"

Biting back a laugh, Megan managed to shrug. "You've been away a long time."

"And while I'm dishing," Rebecca said, leaning closer to deliver her critical, if not downright comical commentary, "what's with Michelle Barante's dress? It's not exactly the purple satin slip thing she wore without a bra to the prom. She looks puffy tonight."

"Well, you would, too, if you were dressing for three. She's expecting twins."

Rebecca delivered a deadpan stare, along with a slow and solemn nod. "That would explain it."

"Let's get Jade in on this."

"Good idea," Rebecca said as they reached out to close their hands around the wrist of the pretty redhead walking by them.

The faraway look in Jade Macleod's eyes suddenly focused on Rebecca and then Megan. She ran a nervous hand over the waist of her black velvet cocktail dress. "Hi, you two. What's happening?"

"We're trying to time travel back to the prom, but reality keeps tripping us up."

"Help us out here, Jade."

After stealing a glance at her escort standing several yards away, Jade gave them a bewildered look. "Why would we want to do that? We're *doing* exactly the same thing we did at the prom."

Megan and Rebecca looked at each other and then at Jade.

"What are we doing?" they both asked.

Jade gave an exaggerated shiver. "We're standing on the edge of the dance floor. Alone. Again. Without men."

Shaking her head, Rebecca gave in to a lively burst of laughter. "She's right, Meggie. We *are* back at the prom." Jutting her chin toward a couple standing several yards away from them, she added, "Listen to that. Lily Magnusson is still arguing with her date."

"I think that's her fourth husband, Reb," Jade said as the couple's arguing got louder, "but my mother told me it's impolite to count them after the second divorce."

As Jade and Rebecca continued the high-spirited repartee, Megan blew softly through her lips as another memory wedged itself into the moment.

When she and Andy used to fight like that, she lived in constant fear that they would be overheard. Even though she'd been widowed over five years ago, she could still recite their arguments line for line. Closing her eyes, she pulled in a deep breath, then swallowed hard. She had looked forward to this reunion for months, and she wasn't going to allow the memory of Andy Sloan to ruin it now that it was here.

"Hey, you two, I have some very good memories of prom night," Megan said.

"You do?" Jade smiled encouragingly as she moved to face her. "We're listening."

"We dare you," Rebecca said, folding her arms across her midriff. "Tell us something that will make us go all gooey."

"Hold on." Megan waggled a finger, as if to stir up a memory. But the memory was already there. Complete, intact, and still shimmering with promised pleasures. "Rory Buchanan almost didn't come because she broke up with her boyfriend the day before. At the last minute, her cousin Nick volunteered to bring her."

Jade shook her head. "Give the lady a ribbon, Reb. I'm actually feeling gooey inside."

"Nick Buchanan," Rebecca said. "Did that guy look great in a rented tux or what?"

"He looked great," Megan said, her heart thumping hard against the inside of her rib cage. She looked out at the crowded dance floor. *He smelled great, too. And when he took my hand and led me behind the curtain of crepe-paper streamers, I began to understand what temptation was all about.*

Megan closed her eyes, her insides tingling at the memory of Nick Buchanan's body pressed against hers and moving seductively to a song that was now a decade old. Maybe it was rubbing up against his bad-boy reputation that still held the power to stir her and her imagination. But was there really any harm in a hardworking widow who was raising her child alone indulging in a sexy fantasy now and then? She pressed her lips together. It wasn't as if Nick was around to tempt her. He had roared out of town on his motorcycle shortly after the prom. She had never seen him again, except in her fantasies.

"Meggie?" Jade asked softly.

Megan opened her eyes to see Jade and Rebecca quietly watching her.

"Are you thinking about Andy?" Rebecca asked.

Megan plastered a smile on her face. A well-practiced smile that she knew would never betray the mixed emotions she felt toward her dead husband. "I'm thinking about when we believed that every dream could become a reality, if we just tried hard enough."

"They still can, Meggie." Jade turned to look at Rebecca. "Don't you agree?" she asked a bit too earnestly.

"Maybe," Rebecca said as she turned a soft smile toward Megan. "If you're willing to be a little flexible with them." A few seconds later her thoughtful expression changed as she looked past Megan. "Look who's coming over. It's Rory."

"We were just talking about you and your gorgeous cousin, Nick," Rebecca said as they welcomed her into their circle. "What ever happened to him?"

Megan held her breath. Her head was suddenly pounding and a wave of panic was threatening to turn nostalgia to nausea. She didn't need to know what happened to Nick. She didn't want to know that he'd probably settled down, gotten married and was developing a paunch while raising his two-point-five children in a heavily mortgaged one-and-three-quarter-bath split-level somewhere in suburbia. Selfish as it sounded, she preferred to remember him as the bad boy who dared to whisper naughty suggestions in her ear while he danced with her in a stolen moment of make-believe.

"Nick moved out to California, but he's never there. His work keeps him on the road."

"That must be hard on his wife and kids," Jade said.

"Nick? Married?" Rory rolled her eyes.

And Megan sighed with relief. At least she didn't have to feel guilty fantasizing about a married man. The last thing she wanted was a dose of reality interfering with one of the few pleasures she had. She still could allow herself the occasional luxury of an innocuous fantasy.

"You know, it's so strange that you asked about Nick though," Rory said. "I had a Christmas card from him last week. He said he's coming back to town next year.''

Rebecca shook her head. "So Follett River's bad boy is finally coming home.''

"Imagine that," said Jade.

Megan stared at all three women, wanting desperately to echo a comparable sentiment. But the breath had left her lungs at the mention of Nick's return.

# One

"**Y**ou married who?!"

Nick Buchanan's casual glance down Main Street careened back to his old friend. The pretty brunette gave him her trademark smile, a mischievous lopsided grin, and the sultry August night was suddenly buzzing.

Rebecca was teasing.

She had to be.

He shook his head. "Reb, you really had me going there for a second. But you always could pull off a good practical joke when anyone least—" He broke off as she lifted her left hand and wriggled her fingers. Her diamond engagement ring and studded wedding band glittered under the street lamp.

"I married Raleigh Hanlon."

Since arriving in the small New Jersey town that

afternoon, Nick had been happily connecting present-day reality with scattered memories. Even after a ten-year absence most of the images were dovetailing easily. This one was decidedly more challenging.

"You married your senior-class history teacher?" He blinked twice. "You married Show-No-Mercy Hanlon?"

She nodded.

"How? When?"

"Earlier this year. I came back for the high-school reunion, and well, things started happening." A faraway look came into her eyes, accompanied by a smile of satisfaction he could only wonder about.

"Well, congratulations," he said with a sincere nod. "You look happy, Reb. That must have been one hell of a reunion."

She laughed softly. "Oh, it was. Remember Jade Macleod? She showed up with a stranger she met on her way there. They're getting married next month. And come to think of it, someone even brought up your name that night." Shaking her finger at him and laughing, Reb leaned closer. "You'd better watch yourself, Nick Buchanan. Coming back to Follett River after all these years could change your life, too."

He gave a playful shudder. "Warning taken."

"Good," she said, glancing at her watch then backing away. "Look, I have to see a man about installing a pool heater, but I'll call you soon. You're staying at the Hotel Maxwell. Right?"

"Yes," he said, before lifting his chin and stilling her steps. "Hold on a second. Whatever happened to that pretty blond friend of yours? You know. The one who'd planned out her whole life. She was dating Andy Sloan, I think.'' He scratched at the side of his head. ''What was her name? Maggie?'' he asked, knowing it wasn't.

''Meggie? You mean Megan?''

He nodded. ''That's it.''

Rebecca studied him for a few seconds, then beamed him a smile. ''Why don't you ask her yourself? She's over at Bailey's. Except it's not Bailey's anymore. It's the Chocolate Chip Café now.''

Rebecca Hanlon stepped into the street and around to her car door. ''Meggie bought the business and turned it into a kind of coffee bar.''

Nick felt his eyebrows lift in surprise. The night he left Follett River Megan had told him a lot of things, but planning to own a coffee bar wasn't one of them.

''Did she ever—?''

''Gotta run, Nick,'' Reb said, cutting him off as she got into her car. ''Oh. Ignore the Closed sign on the door. This time of night Meggie's in the back baking. Just go on in and surprise her. I'm sure she'd love to see you.''

*Love to see me?* He waved as Rebecca drove off. *I wouldn't be too sure about that.* Besides, he really didn't have time for personal visits tonight. Running into Rebecca had been a fluke, and the minutes he'd taken reminiscing with her were already cutting into the hour he'd set aside to study zoning ordinances. Then he thought about the promotion he was being considered for. What he ought to be doing was cutting across the town square to the hotel, instead of thinking about looking up a pretty blonde he hadn't seen in a decade.

Running his tongue along the inside of his cheek, he couldn't help but smile at the memory of the last time he saw Megan. She was standing beside his motorcycle, glaring at him while turning down his offer to relieve her of her virginity.

*"I want a life, Nick. Not just one wild moment I'm sure I'll regret. And, please,"* she said primly, *"don't tell me again what I'll be missing. It's what you'll be missing that should concern you. A safe, secure and respectable life right here in Follett River."*

*She took a step closer and wrapped her fingers around the bike's handlebar. "Nick, I want it to be someone who cares enough to offer me his last name. Not a forwarding address."*

Back then, Nick had recognized the budding signs of Megan's sensual nature even if she hadn't, but at age twenty the last thing he wanted was a white picket fence defining the parameters of his young life. Playing his bad-boy image to the hilt, he'd pulled her into his arms, closed his mouth over hers and begun the hottest, deepest, wettest kiss of his life. When he felt her beginning to respond, he eased away, gave her a "whatever" shrug, then rode off.

He thought about how cavalier, if not downright insensitive he'd acted that night. She was barely eighteen then, and as innocent as they came. He rubbed at his chin, surprised, after all this time, by the trace of guilt still niggling at him. Letting his breath out slowly, he looked toward her café. Hesitation resonated within him.

"Get over it," he murmured, heading up the street. He was thirty years old, not thirteen. She had most likely forgotten the incident. Besides, he thought as he stared at the doorknob, they were bound to run into each other anyway, since he would be in town for the next several months. What would it hurt to stop by and say hello?

The first thing that struck him as he walked inside the shadowed interior was the aroma of coffee and spice and the sense of orderliness about the place. But what had he expected? The lingering smell of greasy French fries? Cola syrup sticking to the bottoms of his shoes? Those No Loitering signs thumbtacked to the walls? Not likely, with Megan in charge.

As he headed for the rectangle of light at the back of the place, he took in the brass-framed posters of European cafés adorning the walls, the ornate cappuccino machine behind the counter and the lavishly decorated desserts in the display case.

This definitely wasn't Bailey's hangout anymore. He stopped at the open door, looked into the brightly lit kitchen and smiled. Not Bailey's by a mile.

A long-legged blonde, leaning over the work surface, was sprinkling powdered sugar across a tray of pastries. Salsa music blared at top volume from a radio just inside the door. Each shake of the sugar can coincided with the beat of the music, while her hips kept time with the rhythm. Firm, curvy, shorts-covered hips. Short shorts. When the music suddenly broke into a conga, she reached to lift her sun-streaked blond hair off her neck. Flexing her knees, she managed an enticing series of bumps and grinds while shimmying her shoulders.

Nick repositioned the pager attached to his belt, then leaned against the doorjamb as the woman continued to do amazing things to his libido. He pictured himself curving his hands around her hips to feel them moving. Or to hold them still. He cleared his throat noisily.

"Can I cut in? Or don't you need a partner for that?"

The instant he spoke, the spirited show ended in an arcing cloud of powdered sugar as she whipped around to face him. She lost her grip on the can, sending it flying across the room. He momentarily lost her in the white swirl.

When the air began to clear, Nick barely noticed the white powder on his shoes; he was too busy admiring the way it was settling on her. From those high cheekbones, all the way to her lightly tanned thighs, she looked as if she'd been hit with a miniature blizzard. Her grape-colored cropped top had moved upward with her jerky movements, revealing a sugar-filled belly button surrounded by flawless porcelain skin.

She squinted under the bright lights, then turned to snatch a cream puff from the tray.

"Who's there?" she demanded, raising the pastry high as if it were a hand grenade. More powdered sugar drifted through the air, but she waved it away.

"I'll give you a hint," he said, taking a step inside the kitchen. He turned down the volume on the radio, then raised his hands in mock surrender. "It's not Elvis."

Her green eyes widened. And those full, soft and lusciously kissable lips parted. The last time he saw her, she had the same expression on her face. He smiled with purely masculine satisfaction, knowing that he could still elicit the same response. And this time, he hadn't even stolen a kiss from her.

"Remember me, Megan?"

"Nick?" she whispered, lowering the cream puff. "Nick Buchanan?" Her disbelieving stare continued for several more enjoyable seconds. Then she laughed.

He remembered her laugh. Flustered and hesitant, the breathy exhalation sounded the same as it had a decade ago when he'd held her in his arms and danced with her at her prom. And right or wrong, for better or worse, he knew why she was the first person he'd asked about on his return. He knew it from the way her laughter still echoed through him.

She shifted her backside against the edge of the table, then nervously licked at the corner of her mouth. A rosy blush continued creeping over her cheeks.

"You surprised me," she said as she tried and failed to maintain eye contact with him. "I—I was just—"

"You certainly were," he said, referring to the sexy dance he'd caught her performing. "And doing a damn fine job of it, too."

When she brushed her fingers across her face and under her chin, he looked for a ring and saw none. *Good,* he thought, pleased beyond measure to know another man's wife wasn't having this stirring effect on him.

In the shared and silent stares that followed, the only sounds came from the hum of the refrigerator, punctuated by the occasional crackle from the bug zapper outside in the alley. The moment shimmered with the almost painful pleasure of knowing he hadn't been wrong all those years ago. Maybe it was revealed at night and only in her kitchen, but Megan's budding sensuality had definitely blossomed.

"You cut your hair."

"You let yours grow."

This time they laughed together and he knew he could easily spend the rest of the night in that kitchen exchanging banalities with her. What did he care about the paperwork waiting for him in his hotel room? Or the dozen or so calls he had to make before his meeting tomorrow night? He'd stumbled on his own welcome-home party and he wasn't planning to leave anytime soon.

"You look good, Megan."

"So do you."

Smiling at her whispered reply, he picked up the can of sugar, took it across the room and set it next to the tray. When he turned to face her, he realized he was close enough to brush the sugar from her forehead...or lick it from her cheek. The thought made his mouth go dry. He leaned his hip against the edge of the table and pointed at the cream puff.

"You have a license to use that, lady?"

"What?" She looked at the pastry in her right hand, then rolled her eyes as she replaced it on the tray.

"So what are you doing here?" he asked, pretending Rebecca hadn't already told him. "Besides making cream puffs to lob at your old friends."

"I bought out Bailey's." Tucking a lock of hair behind her ear, she looked up at him and smiled. "This is all mine," she said, opening her arms, "as long as I pay the rent."

He nodded, noting she was finally beginning to relax a little. "From the looks of things when I walked in, I'd say you bring a lot of enthusiasm to your work. But I thought that Andy Sloan would have had you living in one of those big houses out on Red Oak Road by now,'' he said, referring to the most exclusive area in Follett River.

She looked away, rubbing her thumb against her lips as his gaze drifted over her. The signs of her sensual nature were still there, peeking through as surely as the white satin strap of her bra peeked out of her grape-colored top. Or in the curvy white-blond tempting-to-touch hair tickling at her collarbone. His gaze wandered to her eyes, then drifted downward again. "So whatever happened to Andy?"

"Nick," she said, folding her arms across her midriff, effectively cutting off his view of the taut belly softly punctuated by a sugar-filled navel. "Andy *did* marry me."

Nick blinked, then looked up, his lighthearted mood disappearing in her news flash. She *was* another man's wife; she'd probably removed her wedding band when she'd started to make the pastries. Where was his head? A beautiful, sensual creature like Megan *not* married?

"Whoa," he said, taking a step back. "I *have* been away a long time, haven't I?" He rubbed at the back of his neck, then gave her an apologetic wink. "How is Andy? Still shaking up everyone over at the country club with his tennis scores? Did he become district attorney, like you predicted?"

Megan stared into the darkened dining room of the café. "Nick, Andy died."

If hearing she was married had surprised him, this news threatened to take his breath away. "Megan, I am really sorry. I had no idea."

"That's okay," she said, offering him a forgiving smile before her gaze shifted to the floor.

"How did it happen?" he asked, then wished he hadn't. The last thing he wanted to do was make her feel more uncomfortable by dragging up heavyhearted memories.

"He'd been away on business in the southern part of the state," she said, staring at her white tennis shoes. She crossed one foot over the other and rested it on its toe. "He was driving back and fell asleep at the wheel."

Nick gave a sympathetic shake of his head. What he wanted to do was take her in his arms and comfort her, but that was probably the last thing she wanted from him after he'd just been teasing her about Andy.

Shifting uneasily, he studied her profile, hoping to find a clue for what to do or say next. Her eyes were dry. Her chin wasn't trembling. Her lips weren't quivering. All in all, she was handling the tragedy remarkably well. Come to think of it, he wasn't surprised. Even at the untested age of eighteen, she had impressed him with an unusual strength of character. That same strength was now seeing her through the brittle reality of death.

Closing his hand over her shoulder, he managed, in the process, to tangle his fingers in her silky blond vanilla-scented hair. Those strands of hair might as well be made of steel cables and her shoulder a magnet holding him fast. He swallowed hard. Until that moment, he had no idea how strong his desire was to touch her. "Megan, is there anything I can do?"

Keeping her head bowed, she smoothed the toe of her shoe along an imaginary line on the floor. "It happened a long time ago."

"I see," he said, giving her shoulder a comforting

squeeze while he tried and failed to ignore what her nearness was doing to him.

Looking up at him, she let her gaze wander over his face, as if she were seeing it for the first time. Or memorizing it for the last time. Whatever the case, that glimmer of heated awareness he saw in her eyes was undeniable. So was that tugging sensation low in his belly. "How long ago, Megan?"

She was staring at his mouth now. "This September will be six years."

"Six years," he repeated as vague feelings of guilt scattered to make way for the relief rushing through him. *Six years?* The tension he hadn't realized he'd been holding in his shoulders began to uncoil. He wasn't certain about the protocol on such things, but six years sounded like a long enough grieving period to him. By the look in Megan's eyes, he thought it safe to assume that she did, too.

He lifted a lock of her hair and moved it behind her shoulder. "Six years is a long time to be alone," he said, one breath away from a kiss.

Megan Sloan froze on his last words. That Nick Buchanan had walked in on her while she was in the middle of a wildly sexy fantasy about him was astonishing. That she hadn't screamed, passed out, or worse, tried to start a conga line with him was a miracle. But he'd just sent her crashing to earth with his last remark. She stepped away from the table.

She'd always known what to do with him in her fantasies, but dealing with him in real life wasn't the same. And with everything else going on in her life right now, she did not need more impossible visions of Nick Buchanan crowding her thoughts. He'd taken a piece of her heart when he left town ten years ago. She wasn't about to let that happen again.

Pulling at the hem of her shirt, she made several unsuccessful attempts at covering her navel before she gave up and crossed her arms over it. "I haven't exactly been alone for the last six years."

He leaned an elbow on the worktable and smiled. She remembered that smile so well. Part tease, part challenge, all bad boy and designed to make any woman who saw it melt. That damn smile. He could make curved lips and a riveting stare say more than mere spoken words ever could.

"So what are you saying? Is there someone special?"

"Very special." The sooner Nick knew, the sooner he'd take the next predictable step...like every other man she'd met since Andy died. He'd leave. And she could start to forget that the gap between fantasy and reality had been bridged tonight. "Nick, I was pregnant when Andy died. I have a little girl."

"A little girl?" He blinked as he pushed up from the table. "And you're raising her all by yourself?"

"Aunt Sandra, my mother's sister, watches her during the day, and for that matter, most anytime I need her to."

Megan walked over to the framed corkboard next to the refrigerator. "Her photo's over here," she said, pushing aside several colorful crayon drawings to reveal a department-store photo. The plastic puppy barrettes and infectious grin only added to the charm of her child's button-nosed beauty.

Nick walked up behind her, curved his hand over

her shoulder and leaned to get a good look at the photo.

*My God,* she thought, *I wasn't imagining it before. He's wearing the same aftershave he used ten years ago. A peppery lime scent that smelled like citrus punch on other men and a private party waiting to happen on him.*

Megan held her breath as he reached past her. "What's her name?" he asked as he worked out the plastic pushpin and lifted the photo.

"Paige. She'll be starting kindergarten soon."

"I have to get a better look," he said, taking the photo from the shadowed corner of the kitchen to the bright light over the worktable.

Megan watched him study the picture for a few strangely heart-thumping seconds.

"She's got your hair and that one dimple of yours," he said, nodding as he touched his own cheek. "And she tilts her head like you do."

"Does she? Let me see." She joined him by the table. "You're right," she said, looking up to find him staring at her and not the photo. "I never noticed that before."

His soft laughter made her ears tickle and her breath catch. "She's beautiful, Megan. Are those boys in kindergarten ready for her?"

"Well, I don't know about them," she said, halfway disarmed by the genuine tone of his comments, "but she's ready. She's had her clothes picked out for the first day for over a month. The shoes, she tells me, are another matter completely."

Resting his hands comfortably on his hips, he shifted his weight to lean against the table. "So what's that about?'' he asked, pretending mild confusion over the child's whimsical concern.

He appeared in no hurry to rush out the door. If anything, he looked as if he was enjoying their conversation and wanting more of it.

Taking the photo from him, she tapped it lightly against her palm. A ripple of misgiving moved through her. Was she crazy? Nick couldn't possibly be interested in the domestic details of her ordinary life. Turning away, she headed back to the corkboard.

''She can't make up her mind between her tap shoes and her new red ones. But enough about that,'' she said, firmly securing the photo to the board with the pushpin before turning to face him again. ''You've been away so long, Nick. What brings you back to Follett River now?''

''Work,'' he said, replacing his inquisitive expression with that impossible-to-read smile.

Every time he looked at her or spoke, pangs of pleasure erupted low in her belly, then spiraled out slowly to her breasts and thighs. She attempted to ignore the last and most powerful sensations as she walked back to him, but the closer she got the more intense they became. By the time she reached him, it was all she could do to grab hold of the table and not him.

''I was talking to your cousin at my class reunion last winter,'' she said as she concentrated on her white-knuckle grip. ''Rory said something about you being on the road a lot. What kind of work do you do?''

''I'm in construction.'' He placed his hand on the table next to hers. ''I'm here with the Murano Group for the River Walk project. Have you heard about it?''

"Everyone has. It's the main topic of conversation with us local business owners," she said, trying not to stare at his well-tanned, hair-roughened hand resting on a layer of powdered sugar beside her fair-skinned one. She closed her eyes. Instantly, images of him stripped to the waist and standing in a layer of sawdust slipped unbidden into her mind's eye. With one hand firmly gripped around a piece of lumber, he was hammering nails with strong, even strokes. The scene was taking place out at the old warehouse, the sun blazing across his perfectly tanned shoulders. Rivulets of sweat were trickling down his spine and into the waistband of his jeans. She licked nervously at her lips as she opened her eyes. Her gaze darted from his hands to his face and back again. "I always thought of you doing it, I mean, doing something outdoors."

"I'm indoors a lot, too." A frown that did nothing to diminish his good looks fell across his face as he snapped his fingers. "The business owners' association. That reminds me," he said, checking his watch. "I have a few more things to take care of tonight. Will I see you at the hotel tomorrow night for the meeting the Murano Group is hosting?"

"I'll be there."

"Good. I'll look for you," he said, turning to go. One step toward the door and he slowed to a stop. "Oh." Turning around, he raised his index finger and smiled. "Didn't you forget something?"

He was coming toward her again. Just like before. Ten years hadn't tarnished his appeal. If anything, she was even more attracted to him now. Dangerously attracted.

"What?" she managed to ask.

As he closed the space between them, she reached back with her other hand to brace herself.

"I guess it slipped your mind once we started talking," he said, his deep voice vibrating nerve endings she thought long dead. "That's okay. I'll just help myself."

He kept on coming closer until she was bending backward and he was reaching past her, his arm gently brushing hers. Her lips parted in a soft gasp as his chest grazed the tips of her breasts. A second later he was pulling back with a cream puff in his hand.

"Got it."

"Nick Buchanan," she said with a breathless laugh meant to hide her disappointment. "You haven't changed a bit."

"Don't be so sure," he said, winking at her as he headed for the back door.

The bang of the screen door punctuated his exit as smartly as the flourish of a magician's wand. Megan stood alone in the kitchen, aware of a sudden and immense silence. For one delusional moment, she wondered if she'd conjured up his surprise visit. Then she glanced down at the tray of cream puffs. Nick Buchanan had been there. One was missing. And so was another piece of her heart.

# Two

"Come on, Rebecca," Megan murmured. "You never used to be late to anything. Don't start now."

Pacing inside the Hotel Maxwell lobby the next evening, Megan alternately glanced at her watch, then rimmed its band with her fingertip. Ten minutes and counting until representatives from the Murano Group were scheduled to start their meeting for business owners, private investors and the local media about the River Walk project. Everyone expected to attend the well-publicized meeting had arrived except Rebecca.

And Nick Buchanan.

Megan stopped to look toward the glass-and-brass revolving doors. The last thing she wanted was to run into Nick. It had been almost twenty-four hours since she'd seen him. Plenty of time to sort through and make sense of her reaction to his surprise visit, but not quite enough time to feel altogether comfortable with the decision she'd come to.

Maybe it was a tad excessive, but avoiding a roustabout construction worker who spent his life on the road was the smartest thing a woman in her position could do. The smartest and the hardest.

She tried convincing herself that the thoughts he'd stirred up by his surprise appearance would settle down by the time her radio buzzed her awake the next morning. But the buzz she was experiencing eight hours after his visit had been going on long before her radio alarm.

Enticing dreams about Nick left her feeling as if she were in a modified version of *Goldilocks and the Three Bears*. Tossing and turning in her single bed, the once comfortable piece of furniture was suddenly too big *and* too small.

The truth was undeniable. Nick Buchanan, the bad-boy charmer of ten years ago, the centerpiece of her sexiest fantasies, the man she was losing valuable sleep over, was back in her life and majorly capable of distracting her from her goals, if she let him. She tugged at her watchband. Those fantasies! She had to put a stop to them.

Closing her eyes, she settled both hands over her rib cage and tried pulling in an even, calming breath. Without warning, Nick's naughtiest smile slipped into her mind's eye. The tantalizing rush of pleasure cascading through her a second later caused her lips to part and her resolve to rapidly soften. That naughty smile of his was hinting at something memorable. Nibbling at her lips, she gave in to a luxurious sigh as the vision behind her eyelids began surging to life.

*They were in the café kitchen alone, sometime after midnight. Soft music drifted around them as they made minimal efforts to keep on dancing. Pressed against Nick's masculine form, she felt light-headed with growing desire. After all these years, being this close to him was too much, yet it wasn't enough for her. Sliding her hands down his back, she gazed up at him.*

*"Nick," she whispered, unable to keep the aching need out of her voice. Drawing her nails against the small of his back, she gently nudged him with her hips. "Please, Nick."*

*"You've been alone for such a long time, Meggie," he said as he set her away from him and against the worktable. "I don't want to hurt you. We have time."*

*"I don't want to be alone anymore," she said, brazenly slipping her hand between them to press against the hard evidence of his arousal. "You want me, Nick. I can tell you want me."*

*"Hell, yes, I want you," he whispered on the end of a groan. Staring down at her with half-closed passion-hot eyes, he sealed his lips to hers with a quick, hungry kiss. "Keep touching me like that, and we aren't going to make it to a bed."*

*She kept touching him like that. "I don't need a bed, Nick. I need you. Right here. Right now."*

*Cursing the state of his arousal, he pulled away from her, then swept the worktable clear. Pastry trays were still clattering on the floor as he lifted her onto the edge of the table and began to answer questions she'd only dreamed about.*

Her eyes flew open, then continued to widen as several highly erotic possibilities of what might happen next began forming in the steamier recesses of her imagination. The tips of her breasts, the tops of her thighs and every inch in between tingled.

She looked guiltily around the lobby, scolding herself for thinking about what kind of a lover the real Nick would make. Transitioning into full-time catering to insure a financially secure future was supposed to be the only thing on her mind. Her busy life was complicated enough without Nick, thank you very much. Especially after that letter from her landlord last week, warning her about the rent increases.

Staring at her reflection in a nearby mirror, she shook her head at the jumble of thoughts crowding in. She had to keep herself directed toward goals that could and would come true. Not toward self-indulgent flights of fancy that were getting completely out of hand.

But how had those self-induced visions become so achingly explicit? They weren't inspired by any sexual experiences she'd had. No, sex with Andy had never hinted at anything so...interesting.

She rubbed at her temples. If the reality of Nick was half as potent as the Nick in her fantasies, she could be in trouble. She sighed. Big trouble. Of course, she had no intention of placing herself in a position to find out just how big. Besides, wasn't it painfully obvious that she was anything but a wild, hot seductress? Her lips suddenly thinned with annoyance as she narrowed her eyes toward her reflection.

"Pull it together, Meggie," she mumbled. "Come on, just like you always do when things get dicey. Think about that sweet little girl who needs you. And how nothing is more important than making a better life for her.''

"I heard that mumbling."

"Rebecca!" Megan whirled around to face her.

"Hey, girlfriend, I thought you would have gone in and gotten us seats."

"I told you I'd wait for you here," she said, looking over Rebecca's shoulder toward the revolving doors. Thankfully, Nick was still nowhere in sight. "Where have you been?"

"I'm still on my honeymoon."

"But you were married months ago," she said, taking her by the elbow and drawing her across the empty lobby. "How long is a honeymoon supposed to last?"

Rebecca gave her a devilish grin. "As far as I'm concerned, as long as Raleigh can."

Megan's breath caught in her throat. A second later she was stealing a glance at her friend. Was it true? Was the kind of wild, unbridled passion she'd only imagined really possible?

"Meggie, darling, I always could make your ears turn red. Couldn't I?"

"Your talents know no boundaries, Reb," Megan said, shaking her head with genuine amusement as she reached for the door to the meeting room.

"That's what Raleigh keeps telling me. You want to fill me in on what that conversation you were having with the mirror was all about?"

"No."

"Are you sure?"

"Trust me. Your eyes would glaze over. Let's just go inside and find seats," she said, grabbing two programs from the table near the doors.

As they headed for the front of the room, she couldn't help herself. She made a quick scan of the room looking for Nick. Maybe she'd missed him. Maybe he'd slipped in a side entrance to the hotel. Taking a seat in the front row, she began fanning herself with the programs.

Maybe he wasn't coming. She wouldn't be surprised. If he was anything like he was ten years ago, missing this meeting would be right in character for Nick. She pictured him in his jeans and leather jacket, roaring down the highway to who knew where. Wind whipping through his hair, his thighs tightly gripping his motorcycle, that hell-bent look in his eyes....

She fanned a little faster. He'd probably already forgotten he'd stopped by last night. That would be the best possible thing that could happen. In small-town Follett River, an absence of curious questions would make her plan for avoiding him a lot easier.

"So I hear you had a surprise visitor last night."

The programs crumpled in her grip. She turned to her friend.

"He told you?"

"Well—"

Grabbing Rebecca by the wrist, she leaned toward her and lowered her chin. "He actually told you he caught me dancing by myself in the kitchen?" she asked in a choked whisper.

"Dancing?" Rebecca did a double take, then looked around before she leaned closer. "Meggie, Nick caught you dancing? That's the first I've heard of it."

"Oh." Pulling back, she stared straight ahead. "I'd appreciate it if you'd forget I ever mentioned that," she said, relaxing in her seat as she smoothed out the programs.

"No problem, Megan."

She slapped a program into Rebecca's hand. "Good."

"Right. Thanks. So, then what happened?"

Megan twisted to face her again as someone took the empty seat on her right side. A trousered leg brushed against hers, sending her short skirt higher up her thigh.

"Nothing happened. Absolutely nothing," she said, tugging down her hem as her friend's face lit up with a suspicious smile. "Reb, if you tell one person I told you that, I will never forgive you."

"My lips are sealed." Rebecca raised an eyebrow as she looked past Megan.

"How about you, Nick? Are you going to tell anyone you caught Megan dancing alone in her kitchen last night?"

Megan felt her breath catch in her throat as his arm settled over the back of her chair and the broad and solid wall of his chest touched her shoulder.

"Consider my lips sealed, too," he said, reaching in front of Megan to share a high five with Rebecca.

Megan's gaze slid to one side. His lips were not sealed. They were open in a heart-stealing grin, now fixed on her.

She was trapped between a treacherous friend and temptation powerful enough to make her hands shake. She held back a groan. Why was nothing ever easy in her life? And wasn't it time for someone to strike the gavel? For the floor to open up and swallow her? Or for aliens to beam her up to the mother ship?

She managed to give Nick a closemouthed smile before turning her face to Rebecca. "Give me a break here," she silently mouthed, then quickly looked toward the podium.

"Oh, Nick," Rebecca said in a tone too casual to be believed, "I finally remembered who it was that brought up your name at the reunion."

Megan instantly tensed.

"Who?" he asked.

"You're sitting next to her."

"Is that right?" he asked.

Megan nodded. A moment later she felt the vibrations from the rumble of his soft, deep laughter. The masculine sensation played along every nerve ending in her body, making her feel as if they'd both been laughing. Laughing the way old friends laughed. She tucked a lock of hair behind her ear. Or new lovers.

"What made you think of me?" he asked, leaning his head to fix a curious stare on her.

She managed a shrug as she dropped her gaze to the perfect creases in the trousers of his summer suit. He didn't look like any construction worker she'd daydreamed about. He must have come straight from another meeting. She swallowed hard. Or a date. "I don't remember what made me think of you," she said, moving her leg away from his. That did little to stop the sensation of sparklers sending out their tiny explosions of stinging tickles beneath her skin.

Rebecca leaned closer. "I do. Jade Macleod and I were complaining about the bad time we had at our prom. You know, the one you took your cousin Rory to. Anyway, Megan insisted she had some very good memories from that night."

He rubbed a growing smile from his mouth and nodded. "Yeah. It turned out better than I expected."

It had turned out better than she expected, too. The memory of his tempting whispers and what they'd done to her had her breathing deeply. She smoothed her hand over her leg. *Please, Lord, make him forget we spent all that time behind the crepe-paper curtain, and I swear I'll never...*

He looked at her and smiled. "We did a little dancing. Do you remember?"

"That was such a long time ago."

"Really?" Rebecca asked. "It seems like yesterday to me."

At the sound of her friend's voice, the sparklers gave a sputtering hiss, then died. Lord, was she losing it or what? The man had simply brushed against her and she had been imagining spontaneous combustion under her skin.

Turning away from Nick, she lifted the program from her lap. If she kept her hands busy, she would have a harder time strangling her friend for starting this conversation.

"When I got home last night," Rebecca continued, "I pulled out my yearbook. Raleigh and I spent the rest of the evening looking through it. Nick, did you know that you're in one of the prom photos?"

"No. I'd like to see that."

"I'm going to New York tomorrow morning, but I'm stopping by Megan's café first. If you want to meet me there, I'll bring it with me."

"Sounds great. Seven okay?"

"Perfect." Rebecca closed her hands over Megan's

wrists. "Meggie, stop thumbing through that program and listen."

*Listen?* Her ears were burning! They were coming to the café tomorrow morning and there was nothing she could do about it. And why hadn't anyone started the meeting yet?

"Do you remember your line from the Girls Most Likely to... list?"

"No," she said, giving Rebecca a warning look. "But whatever it was, I'm sure it was way off the mark."

"Not necessarily. You were voted the Girl Most Likely to Surprise Us with Her Secret Fantasies."

Megan managed to stop herself, just before giving in to a full cringe. Everyone, including her, had laughed at that line ten years ago. But she wasn't laughing anymore. Rolling the program into a tight cylinder she tapped the edge on her knee.

"Your point, Reb?" she asked, turning a weak smile toward Nick before glowering at Rebecca again. "And I'm sure you have one."

"Well, who knows?" Rebecca gave an overly dramatic shrug and widened her eyes. "With all this dancing I'm hearing about, maybe you secretly wanted to be a showgirl."

Looking over at Nick, Rebecca kinked a brow. "What do you think, Nick? You've seen her dancing a few times. Has she missed her calling?"

Smiling to himself, Nick checked his watch, then stood up. Bracing his hand on the back of Megan's chair, he leaned in, giving her the momentary illusion that he was going to kiss her. He wasn't. At least, not tonight.

"Could be, Reb," he said, looking directly into Megan's eyes. "Then again, I've eaten one of her cream puffs. That was a mighty tasty experience, too." Before Megan could close her mouth, he went on. "If you'll excuse me, ladies, I have a speech to make." Stepping into the aisle, he headed for the podium.

Those stolen glances she'd sent his way, the way she'd fidgeted, and that one long look that connected deep in his gut were all answers to his prayers. Whether Megan Sloan looked ready to admit it or not, she was as strongly attracted to him as he was to her.

Taking the steps to the stage, he walked across it to the lectern. The crowded room suddenly grew quiet. He knew what most of them were probably thinking. The same thing Megan was. Follett River's notorious motorcycle bad boy, who once enjoyed the dubious distinction of scaring the hell out of every parent of a teenage daughter in the county, was back in town. But what was he doing there?

Picking up the gavel, he twirled the head against the palm of his hand as he looked out at his audience. "Since I already appear to have your attention, I don't think I'll need this." During the light laughter that followed, he set the gavel aside.

"Good evening. Most of you know me. For those of you who don't, I'm Nick Buchanan." Murmurs started again, and he wondered how many different escapades of his teen years were being recounted around the room.

"Yes," he said, nodding. "That Nick Buchanan."

Again the crowd laughed, a little louder this time and a little longer. Even Megan couldn't help herself.

He let the good-natured response continue for a few

more seconds before holding up his hands to quiet the group.

From the corner of his eye he could see Rebecca whispering to Megan. Whatever Follett River's resident rebel spirit was saying was turning Megan's ears an impressive shade of red. Holding back a smile, Nick lowered his hands to close them over the sides of the lectern.

"Back to business. The good people of the Murano Group have asked me to welcome all of you to our program this evening. Before I tell you why they asked me and before I introduce our speakers, I have a few personal remarks.

"First," he said, allowing his drifting gaze to settle on Megan, "let me say that it's a pleasure being back in Follett River. I'm looking forward to getting reacquainted with old friends."

Megan still appeared to be in a mild state of shock that he was the one leading the meeting. Ten years back he would have found that hard to believe, too. Smiling at her, he waited until her green-eyed stare was locked with his. "We have a lot of catching up to do."

Megan's lips parted the tiniest bit.

*That's right, sweet girl, I'm talking about you and me.*

As if she'd read his thoughts, she nervously moistened her lips with the tip of her tongue, then looked down at her program. Her thick blond hair formed a layered curtain around either side of her face, but it was too late. He'd already seen the blush he'd caused. He had no desire to publicly embarrass her with unwanted attention; he'd suffered enough of that in his childhood. Enduring the humiliation of being known as a member of the neediest family in Follett River had nearly destroyed him. It had also, in the end, given him the impetus to move on to better things.

With the finesse of a seasoned politician, he turned his head for a polite cough before continuing. "I'm also looking forward to being job-site foreman on the River Walk project as well as the general liaison between you and the Murano Group." The room hummed again. He arched a brow. "Unless the Murano Group tells me I'm desperately needed elsewhere, I'm here for the duration of this project."

As another ripple of good-natured laughter filled the room, Nick's hand made an involuntary pass over the pager at his hip. What appeared to be a casual gesture had become a second-nature response whenever thoughts about the promotion filtered through. If and when the home office decided to put him in charge of the company's western division, he wanted to be the first to know. He'd worked hard for the position, proving to himself and his boss that he was capable of the challenge. He smiled at his next thought. The strangest irony was that he would probably find out about the promotion while he was here in Follett River, the very place where he once craved recognition and respect.

"If at any time you have a problem, a comment or a question about anything," he said as he scanned the room again, "and I'm sensing by all that whispering out there that you do, feel free to come to me. I want what you want for the River Walk project. A good start to a new beginning for Follett River. So don't be afraid to speak up. I'm here to listen. I'm here to help.

Any time." Playfully shaking his finger at the audience, he let his gaze move back to Megan. "But just remember, turnabout is fair play on any of those questions."

# Three

Early morning sunlight was streaming through the bay window of the Chocolate Chip Café as Megan tamped the ground espresso beans into the portafilter. "So far, so good," she said to herself as she gave the cappuccino machine a warning glance. Wiping her palm against the front of her apron, she went to the machine, slipped the portafilter into place and attempted to secure it with a solid yank. The handle didn't budge.

Pulling it out, she tried again, beginning with a few faint jiggles, progressing to one firm pull and ending with a series of solid jerks. Still no secure connection. Of all times for the gasket to slip! Megan glanced back at Nick. He was sitting nearby with Rebecca and Raleigh, happily poring over Rebecca's yearbook while he waited for his drink.

Megan turned back to jerking the handle. It might have been the Rock of Gibraltar for all it moved. Closing her fingers in a choke hold around the smooth plastic, she leaned her forehead against her wrist and stifled a scream of frustration.

Last night Nick had talked about new beginnings, but how was she going to get to hers if she had to write another check to the restaurant supply company? Gritting her teeth, she returned to jerking as she pictured the two rent checks she had to write out tonight. Rent checks that included the new increases on both her apartment and the café. "Ouch!"

Staring at the tender flesh on the heel of her hand, she swore under her breath, then applied a soothing lick against the reddened indentations. Why was nothing ever easy? she wondered as she shifted her stance and began again from a different angle.

Nick's voice sounded from the end of the counter. "Can I help you with that?"

Her gaze slid toward him. He was casually resting his forearms on the counter, his brows raised in expectation of her response.

*Help!*

But hadn't she sworn she wasn't going to involve Nick in any aspect of her life? Looking back at the brass-and-copper monstrosity dominating the back wall, she quietly groaned. Any minute now, the morning crowd would be coming through the door and demanding their favorite coffee drinks from the list on the wall. Preparing all of them started with an easy pull on the handle of the portafilter. A handle that remained stubbornly immovable.

If this wasn't her busiest time of day, she would

have politely declined Nick's offer. But this *was* the busiest time of day and there was nothing more unpleasant than trying to pacify a mob of caffeine-challenged customers with a penchant for exotic coffees when there were none available.

Squinching her lips, she glared at the machine. What choice did she have? Desperate situations called for desperate measures.

With an odd mixture of defeat and gratitude, she wiped her sore hand on her apron and turned back to Nick. "Do you know anything about cranky cappuccino machines?"

"No, but I doubt beating the hell out of it is going to help," he said, walking behind the counter with a reassuring grin. "Let's have a look."

If she felt closed in by his presence in her kitchen that first night, she felt positively trapped behind the counter this morning. Though lean and well muscled, he was also tall and broad shouldered. And she was having a slight case of hysterical paralysis, all because of a flashback to her prom, when he had brazenly approached her for a dance.

True, his black T-shirt was about as far from a tuxedo as one could go in the world of fashion, but when it came to sex appeal Nick still ruled. Killer grin, faded jeans and all. His masculine presence was as unnerving as it was invigorating. Or maybe that was just the two espressos she'd had this morning before the machine rejected the portafilter.

As he approached, she could think of only one thing. Sharing the small space behind the counter with Nick was going to be more challenging than sharing it with two of her waitresses and little Paige, all at the same time. Quickly checking behind her, she backed herself into the corner next to the machine just before he reached her.

"Okay, Megan," he said, pinning her in place with those big brown bedroom eyes. "What seems to be the problem?"

"I don't—I don't have a problem."

"I'm sure you don't, beautiful. I meant with your cappuccino machine."

"Oh, right. Let me show you," she said, attempting to sound nonchalant while she untangled her fingers from the apron strings tied around her waist. She waited for him to take a step backward before she took a small one forward. Carefully positioning herself in front of the machine, she made certain Nick was behind and to the side of her before she reached for the portafilter and promptly jabbed him in the ribs with her elbow. His surprise exhalation both warmed the back of her neck and made her shiver. Wrestling herself into a tight turn, she didn't stop until she was facing him. "Nick, I'm sorry," she said, running her fingertips over the spot she'd connected with.

He gave her arm a reassuring squeeze. "No damage done."

"Are you sure?" she asked, not wanting to take her hand away from the solid wall of sculpted muscle. "I gave you a good one."

"Believe me, this body has survived worse."

Taking a step away from her, he gave her the room she needed to make an uneventful turn back around to the machine. She'd just started breathing a little easier when he came in close again and lowered his head next to hers.

"This is a tricky position," he said, tucking a lock of hair behind her ear, "but if you relax, I can promise you that neither of us will do anything we'll be sorry for later."

There was a double entendre in there someplace, but she wasn't going to dwell on it now. Using her other hand, she closed her fingers around the handle and tugged.

"See? When I do this, it doesn't budge. The gasket slipped and it's totally locked up."

Before she could step aside, he reached around her with both arms, caging her in a parody of an embrace.

"Like this?" he asked, as he began tugging the handle.

"Exactly like that," she said, closing her eyes as his jarring moves became a masculine force field surrounding her. It would be so easy to melt back against his body and lose herself in the enticing vibrations.

"Nick, I hope you know what you're doing." *Because being this close to you, I don't.*

"Trust me."

"Okay," she murmured, slowly leaning in the direction of his chest. Any millisecond now she'd be quietly reveling in Nick's embrace. From there, anything could happen. Anything she wanted, anything she could imagine...

*"We only have a little while before you have to open the café,"* Nick whispered as he stripped off his shirt and dropped it.

*"How long?"* she asked, turning from him as she frantically worked to undo the buttons on her blouse. *They'd managed to pull the shades and lock the door*

*of the café, but once opening time came people would be banging to get in.*

"Ten minutes."

"Ten? Only ten?" she asked as she shrugged out of her blouse and tossed it unceremoniously atop Nick's T-shirt on the floor.

Laughing against her ear, he reached to unhook the front closure on her bra. "But they'll be ten very action packed minutes," he said, pushing aside the white satin to cup her breasts in his large hands.

She sucked in her breath as his callused thumbs stroked the sensitive tips of her breasts. "Nick," she moaned, pressing her backside against his erection as she reached to grip his thighs. "You make me feel so good when you touch me this way."

He placed one hand low on her belly, then began inching toward the apex of her thighs. "How about this way, Megan?" he asked hotly against her ear.

"How about this other connection? Is it working okay? Megan?"

Her eyes flew open as she bowed her back away from him and reentered reality with a thud. "Th-that one? No. It hasn't worked for a long time."

"That's what I thought," he said, closing his hands over the sides of her waist to guide her to the other side of him. "What do you usually use to loosen this up? Besides your hands, I mean."

Thank heaven his attention was on the machine and not her face, which had to be flaming red about now. She'd almost lost it there for a second. Vowing she wouldn't make that mistake again, she reached under the counter for the cigar box.

"I keep a few tools in this," she said, setting the

well-worn cardboard box next to the machine. "Nick? You will be careful. Won't you? I'm never sure which tool is the right one and I don't want to end up making things worse."

"I've been told I'm surprisingly gentle with these," he said, holding up his hands like a surgeon waiting for his sterile gloves. "Of course, if you're squeamish maybe you shouldn't watch."

"Nick," she said, her voice straining more than she wanted it to, "this machine costs more than my car."

Nick looked at her for a few seconds before giving her a soft smile.

"Meggie, I'm kidding," he said, fishing a pair of pliers from the box, then pulling a clean handkerchief from his back pocket. He stuffed the cloth between the connection and the fancy brass trimming. "If Rebecca and Raleigh aren't totally engrossed in nuzzling each other, maybe you could let them know I'll be a few minutes."

She looked toward their table and saw that all four chairs around it were empty. "Looks like they left," she said as she spied Rebecca's yearbook, their tab and a ten-dollar bill on the counter. "I guess they didn't say goodbye because they didn't want to distract us. Anyway, they left the yearbook."

"Good. I wasn't done looking through it."

Megan slid the book closer, then drew her thumb over the raised gold lettering on the cover. Bittersweet memories from a more innocent time returned to her consciousness, but she quickly stopped them with a little shake of her head. She couldn't think of one reason she would want to revisit that part of her life. As she turned to ring up Rebecca and Raleigh's check, her gaze shifted to Nick. Okay, maybe there was one reason.

"Megan, this could take a while. If you need to do something else, go ahead," he said, never lifting his gaze from his work. "I'll let you know when it's working."

From her vantage point behind the counter, Megan could see that her two waitresses had everything under control out on the floor. She *could* clear off a table or check her supply of clean cups but when would she have a safe reason to be this close to Nick again? She drummed her fingers on the faux marble countertop, then quietly cleared her throat.

"Maybe if I watch how you're doing that, I'll know what to do next time this happens."

"Good idea. Come a little closer," he said, motioning to her.

Moving in, she looked down to where his hands were busy manipulating the gasket. Mistake. Big mistake, she thought as she remembered the scandalous remark Rebecca had whispered to her last night during Nick's welcoming remarks, about the size of his hands in possible relation to another of his body parts. Now she couldn't stop looking at them and thinking...

Nick could have been giving her emergency instructions on how to land a plane in a hurricane and she wouldn't have heard a word. His hands were big, beautiful, and she was fairly certain, fully capable of fixing a few things wrong with her. She swallowed slowly as he spun a loosened fitting with the tip of his finger. He glanced up at her, then back to his work.

"By the way, I didn't see your name on the list of businesses waiting for a space at River Walk."

"Right," she said, reminding herself that she was still determined to keep all aspects of her life separate from him. The last thing she wanted was to start up a relationship with such a tempting man. Before she knew it, he'd be taking her off track from her goal, breaking her heart and blowing out of town shortly thereafter. "I don't have any plans to move over there. The café business depends on the college, the downtown offices, and of course, the shoppers. I'd be crazy to give up that steady flow of customers."

She looked away from him as a whisper of unexpected guilt ribboned through her. Confused and annoyed over her reaction, she felt her brow furrowing. This was ridiculous! No one, including Nick Buchanan, needed to know she was planning to sell the café business and go into full-time catering until she was ready to announce it. She'd made a mistake of boasting about her future plans ten years ago and ended up suffering more disappointment and humiliation than she would ever have thought possible.

"If you're not interested in moving your business to River Walk, then why did you come to the meeting last night?"

She stole a look at him through her lowered lashes. "I do a little catering on the side. I wanted to make sure the promotional material for my catering business didn't get shuffled under someone else's on the display table. You know how it is," she said, stroking her forearm. "If you want things done right, you have to do them yourself."

He looked up and gave her a mischievous wink. "And here I thought you came to see me."

Nick lifted his head just in time to see her looking

away. Smiling, he exchanged the pliers for a small wrench. So she *had* come to last night's meeting because of him. Pursing his lips, he began whistling a soft melody.

He waited until she'd filled an order from one of her waitresses before he spoke to her again. "Tell me about your catering business."

"As I said, it's a side business," she responded as she rested her beautiful behind against the back counter, several sweet inches away from his hand. "It's called Piece of Cake. I've been running it out of the kitchen here for about a year. I cater bridal showers, private receptions, affairs like that."

"Is there much call for that kind of business here in Follett River?" he asked, aware of how her voice and expression had changed once he mentioned the catering business. He hadn't seen her so animated since he found her dancing in her kitchen.

"You'd be surprised how much. Lately, I've actually had to turn down some last-minute requests. And I think I'll have even more business coming my way because of the people River Walk will bring into this area. Word of mouth helps, too."

She reached to touch his arm. "You remember Jade Macleod, don't you?"

"The pretty redhead from all that money? Sure," he said, smiling to himself over his wise or maybe just lucky choice of subjects. Figuring out how to get Megan to relax with him had become a challenge. Had he finally cracked the code? Other than her daughter, was talking about Piece of Cake the way to make her shine that smile his way?

"Jade's getting married next month. She's asked me

to make her wedding cake. Five tiers,'' she said as she pressed her hand to her collarbone and smiled like a kid talking about a new toy. Excitement glittered in her eyes. ''Nick, I've never decorated a five-tier cake before. And listen to this. She wants caramelized stars on the cake. Dozens of them. Doesn't that sound like fun?''

''You bet.''

She opened her mouth to continue, but ended up making a funny face at him instead. ''What am I doing telling you this?'' Shaking her head, she gave into a little laugh. ''You can't possibly want to know about the perils of making stars out of sugar.''

''Yes, I do,'' he said, leaning around her to place the wrench in the cigar box before he closed a hand over her arm. ''Anything that makes you smile interests me,'' he said, keeping his voice purposely low. ''Like I said at the meeting last night, I have a lot of catching up to do.''

''About last night's meeting.'' She looked away slightly flustered. ''You surprised, or maybe I should say impressed a lot of people with your opening remarks. People around here wondered whatever happened to you.''

He smiled to himself, pleased to know he was finally earning the respect he'd once craved from the people of Follett River. But that news was a secondary cause for his smile. By the way she avoided looking at him, he knew her cautious behavior had kicked in again. That was okay. He understood that she probably hadn't been seeing many, if any men since Andy died. He planned to change that. He had already come up

with an idea for how they could spend more time together. And something told him she wouldn't refuse.

"How about you? Were you supri—?" Before he
could finish his question, she'd turned her eyes to the
wall clock.

"Will you look at the time?" she said, closing the
lid on the cigar box and sliding it under the counter.
"I shouldn't have asked you to try fixing that. I won't
keep you another minute, because I know you want to
get out to the site early."

"I've been out at the site since five-thirty. I just
came in to look at Rebecca's yearbook and have an
espresso." *And spend some time with you, sweet girl.*

He gestured toward the machine. "So how about it?
Think you'd like to get your old friend that espresso
now?"

Her eyes widened. "It's fixed?"

"Both fittings."

"Oh, Nick." She raised her hands and for a split
second he thought she was going to take his face in
them and kiss him. Instead she made two fists, then
pulled them to her breastbone.

"You have no idea how much I appreciate this,"
she said, bolting into action. "How can I thank you?"

"Throw in a piece of that chocolate cake I saw over
there in the case," he said, backing out from behind
the counter. "Then I want to ask you something."

A few short minutes later he was holding a demi-
tasse of steaming espresso to his lips and watching as
Megan set a generous slice of cake in front of him.

"Mocha nut with fudge frosting," she said, placing
a napkin and fork beside the plate. "Go ahead. Tell
me what you think."

He stared at the glossy frosting and the chocolate coated coffee beans decorating it, then shook his head. "Something tells me this is going to rock my taste buds."

He forked in a mouthful, savoring the rich chocolate flavors from the instant they touched his tongue until well after he'd swallowed. He shook his head again and moaned as he lifted another forkful to his mouth. "Damn, Megan, you're good. Really good."

She waved off his comically earnest response, but there was something about her smile that told him she was proud of her work and happy that he appreciated it, too. He was more convinced than ever that his plan to spend time with her was, like her cake, a good one. He smiled to himself. Hell, the cake and his plan were more than good. They were superior.

"Megan, maybe you could help me out with something. I've got contracted tenants, local investors and a dozen other interested parties who are going to be dropping in at the site almost every afternoon. I'll also be having scheduled meetings out there in the trailer once a week. It would be easy picking up a couple of boxes of doughnuts every morning to set out next to a pot of coffee. But that's not how the Murano Group does things."

"Uh-huh," Megan said, feeling her ears beginning to twitch. Before Nick could continue, one of her waitresses called out an order for two cappuccinos. "Hold on a minute while I get these."

Thank heaven preparing the cappuccinos took no thought, now that Nick had fixed the problem, because her brain was totally centered on what he was saying. And what he might say. If Nick was going to ask her for catering, she would be crazy to refuse it. Steady fixed-schedule catering work didn't come along that often, and never when she needed the money. Then again, she didn't want to appear too eager and have Nick thinking she was interested in him. *Even if that was sadly true.*

Quickly finishing the cappuccinos, she sprinkled cinnamon over the two cups and set them on the end of the counter.

"You were saying?" she asked, turning back to Nick. He'd finished his cake and was now savoring the last few drops of his espresso.

"I know you're busy with the café," he said, settling the cup onto the saucer, then sliding it aside. He opened his hands and shrugged. "And maybe you wouldn't even be interested, but what would you think about supplying me with a couple of these cakes every day?"

She blinked. "Did you say two every day?"

"Right. Oh, and another thing. I'd need a catered sit-down lunch out there once a week. I'd have to get back to you on what day, but I'd make it a set one."

"Nick, that's quite an offer," she said while quietly telling herself that climbing up on the counter and breaking into a tap dance wouldn't help her business persona. What Nick was suggesting was a bona fide take-it-to-the-bank miracle. Just when she needed her cash flow rejuvenated, he'd come up with this.

"Look, I don't want to pressure you," he said, swirling his fingertip through a dab of fudge frosting clinging to the plate. He stood up and licked his finger. "You did say Piece of Cake is a side business. And that you've had to turn down a few jobs. Maybe you could suggest another caterer.''

Nick reached for the yearbook. "Let me know."

"Nick," she said, closing her hand over his. "Wait. I think, well—yes. I mean, I don't have to think. We could do it." She gave his hand a reassuring squeeze, feeling a few tiny scars on its slightly hair-roughened back before releasing him. "We could do business together."

His brows knitted together over a skeptical stare. "Now, you're not just saying that because I fixed your machine. I don't want you to feel obligated to me."

"No, no, no, no, no. Absolutely not. I'd be happy to do it. And how about a Thermos of fresh coffee to go along with the cakes?"

He was smiling again. That enigmatic gut-grabbing smile that she never could decipher. Had he just set her up? She narrowed her eyes at him and he kept on smiling. Maybe. Maybe not. She didn't care. For the first time since she received the rent-increase notices on her apartment and the café, she was envisioning a light at the end of the tunnel.

"Coffee's a good idea. You can start tomorrow. I'll meet you at the trailer and we can discuss the money then," he said, picking up his hard hat from the table and heading for the door. The little bell jangled overhead as he went out. A second later he opened it again and stuck his head in. "Bring one of those cakes," he said, pointing at his empty plate. "And surprise me with the other."

"You got it," she said as she watched him go a second time. As she cleaned up the counter she told herself that warning tickle at the base of her spine was nothing but leftover excitement. Those cakes weren't cheap. She was about to have steady money coming her way. Piece of Cake would be receiving a lot more exposure. And this was going to remain strictly a business thing between Nick and her.

"Strictly a business thing," she murmured as she reached for a sponge to clean a few crumbs from the counter. Her hand slowed in midswipe.

Just how complicated could this business arrangement become? She nibbled at the inside of her cheek. Getting through this catering job without stirring up anything between them did not require hours in a war room planning a strategy. She would simply drive over to the construction site, deliver the goods, then leave. What was the big deal?

Shaking her head, she twisted around to toss the sponge into the sink. Honestly, she amazed herself at how easily she borrowed trouble. What could possibly happen between them for a few minutes each day out at a construction site thick with workmen and work?

She must have been crazy when she agreed to this…this self-imposed torture.

Megan sat in her delivery van, smoothing her moist palms along her thighs as she stared at the door to the construction-site trailer. It was just a door that led into an air-conditioned office, she told herself. Not into hell. Not…well, not into heaven, either.

Reaching for the door handle, she ended up slapping her hand over the steering wheel instead. Blowing a sharp stream of air through her lips, she drummed her fingers along the frayed leather casing. What was her problem?

For one very profitable week she had been delivering on her contract with the Murano Group. And for that same very tempting week she'd been doing her best to deal with Nick. Well, with her attraction to him.

That he had been relating to her as the quintessential businessman and perfect gentleman should have made that dealing a whole lot easier. On the contrary, his good manners made him somehow harder to resist. Her attraction to him impossible to ignore. And her sanity suspect when she sometimes found herself wishing for the return of the bad boy she knew was there behind those eyes. Those big, brown bedroom eyes....

"Megan Sloan, you have no time for this. Just get in, get out and get on with it," she said as she opened the van door and stepped onto the ground.

A few minutes later she was entering the trailer with two cake boxes, a coffee Thermos and what she hoped was a convincingly breezy attitude.

Nick was hunched over paperwork at his desk. Not that it mattered. He could have been standing on his head in the corner and she would have felt that same deep pull in her belly she'd been experiencing every day at this time for a week now.

"Megan." Tossing his pencil aside, he laced his fingers behind his head and leaned back in his chair. "What have you got for me today?"

There it was, the cordial and now familiar tone he could have been using with any friend. Or stranger. That was fine. That was how she wanted things between them. No, she thought as she set her things on the table, that was not fine. That was simply how she needed things between them.

"Walnut spice and pineapple cheesecake." She should be grateful he was making this easier. "They're already sliced." By now he probably understood what her life was like. "I have paper dividers separating the pieces." He was doing them both a favor. The least she could do was get control of her heartbeat while she supplied him with all this vital information, which was highly visible and right before his eyes!

Ah, yes. Boring conversation and plenty of it. She would keep slathering it on like butter on a hard roll and hope she was burying any chance of saying or doing something really stupid. Like riveting her gaze on that skin-on-a-grape T-shirt he was wearing today. One glance as she walked in the door had already told her that his broad chest had taken the Murano Group logo and turned it into a blazing white banner across the front of that black T-shirt. The soft cotton defined every rock-hard muscle and every corresponding contour below his wide shoulders and between his beautifully bulging biceps.

When she heard his chair spring creak, she pictured him stretching out his legs, lifting his hips and moving that tight blue-jeaned behind of his into a more comfortable position.

"Presliced and with individual paper separations. Sounds great," he said as she heard the chair skid backward. He was standing. Her heart was pounding again. Now he was walking. Closer. And she was taking in extra oxygen through her open lips.

"Nick, about the menu for next Wednesday's lunch," she said, hurrying to the refrigerator on the other side of the trailer. "Unless you have another idea, I think hot chicken puffs, a mixed salad with mustard vinaigrette and—I don't know, possibly a peach cobbler for dessert. Is that okay with you?"

"Anything you do is okay with me, Megan."

Yanking the fridge door open, she pretended great interest in the contents of the interior. "Gee, look at this. I thought I put two containers of half-and-half in here yesterday. I can't imagine what happened to them. Can you?"

Nick walked up beside her and rested an arm over the top of the refrigerator. "I used one to feed that stray cat that's hanging around. Megan?"

"I'm disturbing you. Aren't I?"

"You certainly are, but not in the way you think."

"What?"

He gave her a lopsided grin and shook his head. "You've been coming out here for a week now, and all we ever talk about are things like Colombian coffee versus Jamaican coffee. Or what size paper napkins go best with cake." Propping his chin with his hand, he gave an enormous sigh as he studied her closely. "Do you suppose, if we try, we could find more interesting subject matter?"

She kept her eyes fixed on the center of his T-shirt as she struggled to think of a safe subject. The wall clock's ticking was starting to sound like a schizophrenic snare drum. Crossing her arms tightly across her middle, she cleared her throat. "That was kind of you to feed the cat, but aren't you afraid you won't be able to get rid of it when you leave?"

"Why would I want to get rid of it? It helps keep those pesky field mice away from the lumber."

"Oh," she murmured as she continued staring at his T-shirt. Her fingers tingled to press against the thin material and feel the heat she knew was just below it. She lowered her eyelids, imagining the solid resistance her fingers would meet with, along with the strong, steady beat of his heart. Without thinking, she stroked her thumb across the words stitched on the pocket of her blouse. Once. Twice. The third time she was half-way across the scrolled letters of Chocolate Chip Café when Nick spoke.

"Nice blouse."

She pulled her hand away to tuck it beneath her arm. Heaven help her. What was she doing? "I was happy to see you decided not to cut down those old oaks near where the river bends."

"The Murano Group does its best to please."

She fought back a smile. Oh, he could definitely please her. "Sounds like you're working for a good company."

He nodded. "The best. If the weather cooperates we'll likely bring this project in ahead of schedule."

"I see," she said, feeling a sudden chill that had absolutely nothing to do with the open refrigerator door. She shut it anyway, and stared across the room. His nicked and scarred hard hat rested on the edge of his desk. She wondered about its history, and more importantly, its future.

"And then it's off to where, Nick?" she asked, hating herself for missing him already.

He shrugged and moved a little closer. "There's plenty of time to think about that later. Meanwhile…"

Guiding her chin with his fingers, he turned her face up to his until she was looking at him.

"Meanwhile?" The soft, throaty sound she produced was only a whisper of what she'd meant it to be.

"Meanwhile…" He slipped his hands around her waist. "I've been looking forward to this for quite some time."

She thought of half a dozen options to stop what she knew was coming her way. But she wasn't going to exercise any of them. Not with that sexy look he was giving her. Her lips parted. There was no way she was getting out of this trailer or this life without a kiss from Nick. But just one.

The decision to accept his kiss was surprisingly liberating. She wasn't going to have to think about it, lose sleep over it or fear it anymore. Her fantasy man's kiss was about to become real.

Moistening her lips, she inched forward. As long as it would be just this one kiss, she might as well abandon herself to it and revel in the relief she knew it would provide.

"Then do it," she said, suddenly feeling empowered by the electrifying look he was giving her.

Her response appeared to surprise him, but it didn't slow him down. Taking her two steps sideways to the corner of the room, he braced his hands against the walls and leaned in close to her lips. He made a move to skim them with his, but lifted his mouth a split second before he touched her. Her breasts were rising and falling more quickly now as he maneuvered his face next to hers in slow-motion moves meant to tease.

"Nick."

"You do it," he whispered.

With an exasperated sigh she sank her fingers into

his thick, dark hair and brought his mouth to hers. That was all he needed. The instant she sealed her lips to his, she felt his hands come off the wall as he wrapped her in a claiming embrace.

Her breasts flattened against his chest as their bodies became dedicated allies to their kiss. Hot, hungry and hell-bent for satisfaction, they moved together as if they'd practiced for this moment all of their lives.

The kiss went on, slowing at times to sweet, luscious nibbles, then deepening with darker, richer need. It was the most glorious, passionate thing that had happened to her since the last time he'd kissed her ten years ago. But this time was different. This time she'd started the kiss, and this time she was milking it for every drop of wanton pleasure. Breathing in the scent of sawdust, his aftershave and the essence of his masculinity, she reached behind him to pull his hips against hers.

She'd barely skimmed his buttocks when the kiss was suddenly over. Not because she'd come to her senses and pushed him away, but because Nick had pulled back. Gasping for breath, she pressed her fingers to her lips. The move was meant as much to hold on to the sensations of the kiss as to stop herself from crying ''more.''

As he returned his hands to the wall behind her, he dropped his head back to look up at the trailer's low ceiling. A few seconds later he pulled in a deep lungful of air, let it out, then looked down at her and smiled.

''Ten years ago, sweet girl, I stole a kiss from you,'' he said as he reached to take her hand away from her mouth.

"Yes, you did," she whispered while his fingers played over her lips. .

"Well, you can't pretend I stole this one."

"You're right. This one was all my fault."

"Fault?" He dropped his head back again and laughed with gusto. "You make it sound as if we'd committed a crime." He shook his head. "I want to see you, Megan. I know that you want to see me, too."

They hadn't committed a crime. She had just made a mistake. A very big—better than she could have imagined—bone-melting mistake that left her jaw muscles quivering, her body moist and needy and the both of them on the fast track to romance if she allowed it. But she wasn't going to allow it. She did not need a short-term fling stirring up her ever-more-complicated life, even if every fiber in her body was screaming for it.

"We do see each other. Every day."

"I'm not talking about over the counter at the café or out here where anyone can walk in. I want to spend time with you," he said in a patient voice while he drew delicate patterns with his fingertip over her eyelids and down her cheeks. "I'm guessing by that reluctant look that you haven't seen many guys since Andy died."

"Not many." *And none worth mentioning.*

He nodded. "Well, we'll take it slow. We'll do this any way you want. Go into New York to see a show. Take in a movie down on Main Street. Have dinner at my hotel. You name it."

She smiled at his determined yet considerate nature and at her own stupidity. Had she really believed that Nick would accept the first flimsy excuse she could

think up, then never ask her out again? She closed her
hands over the enticing muscles in his forearms and
leaned back against the wall. There was really only
one thing to do to get past this temptation and that
was to appear to go along with it. The sooner Nick
realized what her life was about, the sooner he would
back off and let her get on with it.

"Why don't you come to dinner at my place this
Friday? We'll have to make an early night of it,
though, because I take the morning shift at the café
on Saturdays."

"I accept. And you can kick me out anytime you
want," he said, cupping her cheek in his callused
hands. Bringing his face close to hers, he whispered,
"But you won't have to, because I make it a point
never to overstay my welcome."

That was just it, she thought as she joined him in
another kiss. Once he was there, she might not want
to kick him out.

# Four

The miniature green-eyed angel staring at Nick from across the living room had him laughing softly. "I thought I saw a strong resemblance in the photo you showed me, but it pales next to the real thing. Megan, she's so much like you..." He shook his head and smiled at the little girl who seemed reluctant to come any farther into the room.

"Some people say she has Andy's jaw," Megan said, setting the flowers aside that he had just given her. She picked up a framed photo from the entry-hall table and held it out to Nick. "Don't you think so?"

He glanced at the table and quietly noted that there were at least half a dozen other photos of Andy Sloan prominently displayed there. Tucking his package under his arm, he took the picture Megan was offering.

It was a standard wedding pose of a bride and

groom on the steps of a church, but Nick found himself studying it with strange intensity. Andy, in his dove gray cutaway, was smiling proudly at the camera and Megan in her billowing white gown was looking happily at her new husband. Or was she? What was it about Megan's expression that made him pause? Was it hope? Or did he see a trace of unsureness somewhere in that fixed stare? Annoyed for thinking such a disparaging thing, he hastened to remind himself that most brides probably had that semianxious aura about them. And what did it matter when the photograph was already fading?

He looked across the room at Paige. "Andy's jaw? Could be, but honestly with that hair and those green eyes," he said, returning the photo to the table, "all I see is you in her."

Megan opened her mouth to speak but instead smiled, as if she'd suddenly decided not to pursue the issue. Picking up the flowers, she motioned him into the living room.

"Brace yourself," she said under her breath. "She has more energy than I can muster after three cups of espresso." Looking across the room at her daughter, Megan raised her voice to a normal level. "Come on in and say hello to Nick."

Paige looked away as she wound a bright orange string of yarn around her chubby fist. A moment later a stuffed toy slid into view from behind her.

"Momentary shyness," Megan explained under her breath. "This will pass very soon."

Nick nodded. With three younger sisters of his own and too many nieces to count, he'd had plenty of experience with little girls Paige's age.

"You remember I told you Nick was eating dinner with us tonight."

Paige turned her big green eyes to him, gave him a suspicious once-over and reluctantly nodded.

"Nice shoes, Paige," he said, jutting his chin toward the pair of black satin high heels the child was wearing. Nick didn't miss the smile twitching at the corners of her rosebud mouth.

"Do you ever let your mother borrow them?"

Paige giggled as she planted one hand on the wall next to her and the other on her hip. "They *are* my mom's. She says she doesn't ever use them anymore, so I'm borrowing them. I can walk in them. Wanna see?"

Before Nick could answer, Paige began a slow shuffle from the back hallway into the living room. Her teetering gait veered left, then right as she checked over her shoulder at the stuffed animal she was dragging behind her. When the dog fell to its side, Paige reached to set it upright. The twisting move threw her into an off-balance spin that dropped her softly to her fanny. Tears of embarrassment threatened.

And Nick knew just what to do.

"Paige," he said, raising his voice but keeping it calm. "What's your dog's name?"

"Oh." Her quivering pout disappeared. "He's not a real dog," she said with the earnestness only a five-year-old could supply to the obvious. Kicking the shoes aside, she picked up the toy and headed toward Nick. "You wanna pet him? He doesn't bite."

"Well," Nick said, lowering himself to his haunches. "You sure about that?"

"Uh-huh."

"Okay," he said, petting the toy as if it were real. "Got a name for him?"

"Beans. When I get a real puppy I'm gonna name him Beans, too." She pointed at the package tucked beneath Nick's arm. "What's that?"

"It's a present for you."

The little girl brushed her bangs aside and looked up expectantly at Megan. So did Nick.

"Can I have it?" she whispered.

Megan nodded.

With a rushed and obligatory "thank you," Paige took the package he held out to her, sank to the floor and began peeling off the pink elephant wrapping paper.

"Crayons. Oh, Mommy, it's the big box," she said, opening it to sniff at the rainbow of colors inside. A moment later she reached for the coloring book that had slipped from the package. "It's Power Princess," she said before throwing her arms around Nick and hugging him.

"Heather doesn't have this one," she said, looking up at Nick.

"Heather's her friend," Megan explained.

"I'm gonna go color. You wanna color with me, Nick?"

"I was hoping you'd ask me."

"Good." Scooping her gifts from the floor, she turned to go as pink-and-white wrapping paper fluttered around her. After a second's hesitation she turned back to Nick, sending her little pigtails swinging like golden tassels against her cheeks. "Only, just don't color the ones with Power Princess in 'em," she said, shaking her little index finger. "Okay?"

"Okay," he said. "Why don't you pick out two pages we can color on together?"

"Yeah!" she exclaimed, before making a beeline for the coffee table.

Picking up the wrapping paper, he stood and looked at Megan. "Well? How did I do?"

Megan gave him a disbelieving look. "You couldn't have chosen better. It's her favorite cartoon character."

He shrugged. "My cousin Rory's daughter is five. She runs around her house in a Power Princess nightgown. I figured that was a safe bet," he said, peering over the sofa at Paige as Megan took the paper from him.

"And these?" she asked, holding the flowers close to her nose. "How did you know peach is my favorite color for roses?"

Paige chose that moment to call out from her place at the coffee table. "Come on, Nick. I gotta real good picture for you to color. It's a airplane."

Nick winked at Megan. "Better put those in water before they wilt."

When Megan tried to question him again, he made a scooting motion with his hands. "Please. I have an airplane that needs my attention."

After the airplane, Paige found three more pictures for him to color. And he found out all sorts of information from the bubbly little charmer. As Megan finished preparing dinner, Nick learned it was okay to color outside the lines if he didn't do it too often. That Paige's main goal in life was to have a puppy with a pink tongue. Nick asked if there was any other kind. She told him she wasn't sure about that. Nick also learned that Paige was going to be the flower girl at Jade Macleod's wedding.

Listening to the five-year-old's enthusiastic delivery on any and all of those facts would have made him smile, but the one that kept him grinning was the one he never expected to hear. According to Paige, her mother had decided that very afternoon to take photos from a box in the back closet of her bedroom and set them out on the entry-hall table.

Until Paige had told him about this spur of the moment redecorating, he'd been trying to reconcile Megan's photographic exhibition of Andy with the exhibition of her passionate side out at the trailer. Perhaps he was one impure thought away from being a rutting maniac, but he was finding it impossible to imagine Megan's warm, lush body inspiring visions of a bereaved widow in any man's eyes. Now he understood she still had lingering doubts—and maybe even fears—about dating again. One thing, though, he was going to have to make clear to her. He had refused to compete for her affections when Andy was alive. And he refused to compete for the same now that Andy was dead.

Nick was teaching Paige a camp song about gophers when Megan called them to dinner ten minutes later. She didn't know if Nick had an endless supply of patience or was simply determined to impress her with his willingness to submit to the capricious nature of her five-year-old. Either way, her daughter's rapt attention to her new coloring partner was enchanting to witness. It was also cause for pinching guilt.

Like any single mother, Megan had been heart-wrenchingly aware of her child's natural need for male attention. But she'd never seen it manifested quite like this before.

As Megan watched quietly from the other side of the table, Paige propped her chin in her hand, patted her mashed potatoes with her fork and looked adoringly at Nick. All the particulars that made the easygoing man so attractive to Paige were also the things that could break the little girl's heart. The last thing she wanted was for her daughter to form an attachment to him, only for the little girl to see him vanish from her life.

Paige leaned across the table to tap Nick on the wrist. "How come you build things?"

"Well, I had a motorcycle accident a long time ago. After I moved away and before you were born."

Megan's heart skipped a beat. "I didn't know that," she said softly. Nick glanced her way and nodded before turning back to Paige.

"I was in the hospital with a man named Mr. Murano."

Paige tilted her head, and with childlike logic asked, "Did he have a motorcycle accident, too?"

"No, he had a skiing accident. But we both had bad knee injuries and we had to learn to walk again."

"Like Heather's baby brother?"

"Probably. Mr. Murano and I made a game of it. We each wanted to be the first to walk."

Paige laughed. "Did you win?"

Megan leaned forward, wishing in one part of her mind that she didn't find his story so compelling and knowing in another part that anything about Nick would fascinate her.

"In a way we both won, because we helped each other to try. By the time I got out of the hospital Mr. Murano and I were friends and he hired me to work for him. That's why I build things."

Paige nodded, and without missing a beat launched into her next question. "Did you know my daddy?"

Less than an hour ago, Megan might have welcomed the question in her selfish haste to encourage Nick's hasty exit from her life. Now, she only felt a knot of guilt coiling in her chest. She reached to her lap and began wringing the life out of her cloth napkin.

"I met your daddy a few times," Nick said as he glanced at Megan.

"Did you used to play with him?"

"No, Paige, I didn't."

"Why not?"

"Because your daddy and I had different friends."

In the blissfully quiet moments that followed, Megan thought about the photos of Andy that she'd set out that day. What she'd thought was a well-orchestrated move to discourage Nick's attention was turning on her like Frankenstein's monster. Why hadn't it occurred to her that all those pictures would plant thoughts of an absent father in Paige's little mind? Involving Paige in her ploy was never her intention. She could give herself a swift, hard kick on her backside for not thinking this through better.

"More peas, Nick?" Megan asked, hoping to turn the conversation in a different direction. She picked up the bowl and was about to offer them to Nick when Paige began speaking again.

"Nick, did you ever play with Mommy?"

"I tried a few times, but she always had to be someplace else." He turned a tantalizing grin to Megan. "Remember?"

Her gaze locked with his, as visions of them dancing at the prom stole into the moment. She remembered…his hot lips glancing off her neck…his broad hands spanning her rib cage…the tips of her breasts tightening to his touch…her lips parting with a whisper soft sigh.…

Suddenly, the bowl slipped from her hand and peas were rolling across the table in every direction. Nick reached to stop them at the edge, but it was too late. They were already bouncing on the rug.

Paige allowed one reflexive "uh-oh," but as the two adults scrambled to the floor her questions kept on coming.

"But you're Mommy's friend now. Right?"

"You bet," Nick said, heading around the perimeter of the table on his hands and knees.

"Mommy? And now you're Nick's friend. Right?"

"Yes, sweetheart. I'm Nick's friend," she said as she pulled the empty bowl from the table and set it on the floor. Concentrating on gathering up the spilled peas and dropping them into the bowl as quickly as she could, she let out a scream when Nick's face appeared from underneath the table with the white cloth draping either side of his handsome face.

"Does that mean we can play together?" he asked.

Slamming her empty hands to her chest, she rocked back on her ankles and laughed out loud. When she could catch her breath, she wiped tears from her eyes. With that silly grin and his lack of self-consciousness, she knew he had to be the most delightful man she'd ever met. On impulse she leaned in to give him a peck on the cheek. He turned his face at the last moment to press his lips to hers. The kiss lasted a few seconds too long to be categorized as simply a friendly one, but that still didn't stop her from smiling as she drew back. Knowing in that precious and funny moment that she was coming dangerously close to changing her future plans about Nick, she shook her finger in teasing warning.

"Mommy? Are you and Nick playing together now?"

Paige's question came from the other side of the table, but it could have come from inside her own head. Megan looked at Nick and sighed. Precious and funny moments were just that. Moments. Not something to base important decisions on. "We're supposed to be picking up peas," she said, evading Paige's question and Nick's dazzling smile as she reached for more peas.

An hour later Nick pulled open the door and stepped out onto the second-floor porch. "It didn't work, by the way."

"What didn't?" she asked over the sounds of a Power Princess video playing in the background. Nick's smile was a long time coming, but when it arrived her heart took an extra beat, then slipped into panicky misfires.

"You thinking an evening spent with your five-year-old would put me off." He shook his head. "Paige could charm the stripes off a zebra. You're doing a great job with her."

She looked away as he smiled. Why couldn't he

have been angry with her when he'd discovered her ploy? Why did he have to sound as if he were playing a game with her? "Nick," she began as she led him toward the steps, "this night isn't going to change—"

He stopped them both in their tracks. "Megan, listen to me," he said, his voice deepening with a seriousness that made her want to cry. "I know you feel this pull between us. I knew it long before that kiss *you* started out at the trailer. I saw it in your eyes the second we looked at each other. There's something happening between us, Megan. You want to tell me why you're trying so hard to push me away?"

"Nick, I lead an extremely busy life," she said, looking every which way but toward him. "I'm raising a five-year-old all by myself. Some days I end up running the café alone. I hardly have a minute to breathe."

"I know that," he said, gently closing his hands around her shoulders. He waited until she looked up at him before he went on. "I also know that some nights you dance alone in your kitchen. That tells me you have faith in the future, in your hopes and dreams. Let me in on them, Meggie," he said, looking into her eyes.

Her hopes and dreams. She winced when she remembered that uppity speech she delivered to Nick a decade ago about her hopes and dreams. How different her life had turned out. "Nick, you just don't understand."

"No, I don't," he said, smoothing his palms over her arms. "But doesn't it mean something to you that I want to?"

When her chin began to quiver he had the good

grace to close his arms around her and rock her gently in his embrace. No one had held her with such tenderness, such sweet care in a long time. Closing her eyes, she turned her face against his chest and quietly acknowledged the truth to herself. No one had ever held her like this. No one had ever made her feel so safe, yet so close to danger. And it felt so good she never wanted him to let go.

After a while, he drew back to look down at her. "You think you could talk Paige into letting you have those high heels back?"

"Why?" she asked, secretly thumbing a tear from her cheek before she looked up at him.

"Because now that we can play together, you're going to need them next Friday night."

"Oh, Nick," she whispered as he stroked her hair and smiled patiently at her. She turned her face from him, trying her hardest to add determination to her voice. "Tonight wasn't supposed to turn out this way. I thought if you saw what my life was like you'd—"

He turned her face to his. "I'd what? Give up?" he asked in a fierce whisper. "Listen, sweet girl, I'm not about to rush you into anything you're not ready for, but we're not two groping kids at the prom anymore. We're adults."

"I can't promise you this is going anywhere," she said even as she felt her resolve to stay clear of him slipping lower on her list of priorities.

"We'll take this as slow as you want. I'll give you all the space you need." He kissed the tip of her nose. "You lead the way, Megan. We start and stop when you say. Only don't tell me you don't want to see me because we both know that's not true," he said as he continued to hold her face in his splayed fingers. Looking into her eyes, he delivered a request in a whisper that reached down to the loneliest part of her heart. "Say it, Meggie. Say it isn't true."

Closing her hands around his wrists, she gave in to a smile. Defeat had never felt this good before. "It isn't true," she whispered right before he pressed his lips to hers.

# Five

**M**egan expected to encounter Nick at every turn during the following days before their date, but true to his word, he was allowing her plenty of space. Space she was finding as troublesome to deal with as his daily presence had been the week before. If his avoidance of her was also a ploy to make her feel lonesome for him, it was working. Much as she hated to admit it, she missed his genuine compliments about her work, his teasing remarks which made her laugh along with him. Most of all, she missed those blatantly sexy looks that had her both melting and shivering at the same time.

On Tuesday she wondered if she was experiencing a kind of withdrawal from his addictive presence. By Wednesday night she was certain of it, when she arrived at Jade's bridal shower only to realize she'd forgotten to bring her gift. She barely made it to noon on Thursday before she gave in to her desire to see him.

As she lifted cake boxes from her delivery van, she called out to the first workman she saw to ask if he knew where Nick was. The man lowered his wheelbarrow long enough to point to a dozen workers pounding roofing nails on top of River Walk's main structure.

"He's not your usual site foreman," the man explained. "He's a hands-on type."

Megan nodded. She'd never seen Nick shirtless before, but she picked him out from the others before she had time to blink. His bronzed, beautifully muscled torso glistened under the blazing sun, exactly the way it had in her fantasies. She could have stood in that dusty parking lot all afternoon, drinking in the sure and graceful way he twisted and stretched his magnificent body as he worked. Each time he stood up or moved along the pitched surface, she felt as if she were watching a well-choreographed ballet of man, muscle and magic.

When he suddenly turned her way and waved, the cake boxes began to buckle in her tightening grip. Once she made it to the trailer, it took her ten tedious minutes to repair the damage she'd done to the frosting. And another ten before she got up the nerve to make a run for her van.

Returning home from the sitter's with Paige that night, she found a toy-size doghouse on her doormat. Complete with working window shutters, a red shingled roof and *Beans* painted in easy-to-read block lettering over the arched opening, she knew without being told that Nick had made it. After she hauled the miniature structure into Paige's room, she asked her five-year-old to help her search for a card. An ecstatic Paige gleefully informed her mother that she knew who had given her the doghouse.

"Who?"

The little girl opened her hands and gave a dramatic shrug. "Santa Claus. Cause don't you remember? You said sometimes Santa's late, but he never forgets."

"I did, didn't I?"

"Uh-huh. And Nick said so, too," Paige replied as she dropped to her knees to further inspect the new home for her favorite stuffed animal. "Oh, Mommy, isn't Santa wonderful?"

"He certainly is," Megan said as she watched her daughter scooting to the side of the house to peer into a window opening. A part of her wished that Nick was present to witness Paige's unbridled delight. Another part was grateful that he wasn't. The anonymous delivery meant that Paige didn't have to think Nick was the greatest thing to come into their lives since Christmas. Even if Megan had begun to suspect that he was.

Nick had thought about taking Megan to New York City, but quietly congratulated himself for choosing the razzle-dazzle world of Atlantic City instead. He had a feeling Megan hadn't had an evening away from her everyday world in a long time, and the East Coast gambling mecca's carnival-like atmosphere was as far away from motherhood and Main Street as he could imagine. He was saving New York City and that romantic carriage ride through Central Park for later.

His sense of satisfaction began slipping away shortly after dinner, when they walked across the lobby of Crown's Casino toward the Royal Room. As he checked on their reservations for the nightclub's nine o'clock show, Megan was alternately fidgeting with her evening bag and staring at the poster outside the door. By the time they were seated and the waitress had brought their drinks, Nick knew something was terribly amiss.

"If that lipstick is so tasty, think I could get a nibble of it, too?" She slipped in one more quick lick, then gave him an apologetic smile. "Are you worried about being so far away from Paige?"

Megan shook her head. "No. She loves staying with Aunt Sandra."

"Megan, is there something you want to tell me?"

"Well. I, uh…" Nervously brushing at her bangs, she turned her gaze away from the curtained stage and back to him. "No." She shook her head to emphasize her answer.

Taking her hand between both of his, he was surprised at how cold it felt. "I asked you out so that we could both enjoy the evening together," he said gently. "And you're definitely not enjoying much of anything. What's happened? What's on your mind?"

"The…doghouse," she said, removing her hand from his. She smoothed one slim shoulder strap and then the other on that dynamite dress.

He pulled back, arched his brows and made what he hoped was a comical face. "The doghouse?"

"Admit it," she said, forcing a laugh into her voice as she lifted her index finger in his direction. "It was you who left it."

Nick knew that the mystery of who had left the doghouse on Megan's doorstep wasn't what had her so antsy. He also knew that as long as he kept her talking, sooner or later she would stop avoiding the real issue. "It was," he said with a simple, single nod. "How did Paige like it?"

"I haven't seen her this excited since Christmas. I found her curled up beside it with her pillow and blanket this morning," she said as she glanced around the room, then back to him. "She thinks Santa brought it."

"Good," he said nodding again. "That's what I wanted her to think."

Her sparkling green-eyed gaze searched his face. "You did?" she asked, tilting her head just enough to send a pale lock of her hair skimming across the most beautiful cleavage he'd ever seen. "Why?"

As the sultry notes from the saxophone began floating around them, he shrugged. "Everyone needs a surprise now and then. At Paige's age, what could be more fun than a gift out of season from Santa?"

Her eyes locked with his, and it was as if her uneasiness of a few moments ago never existed. When she turned her radiant smile on him, that fragile connection that had been growing between them for the past few hours was back and blooming.

She leaned in close. "And all this time, I thought you might still be that bad boy I used to know," she said with a teasing sparkle in her eyes.

"Oh, don't let this silk tie fool you. I'm still him," he said, letting his gaze drift slowly over the low square-cut neckline of her cocktail dress. The creamy light swells of her breasts made an enticing contrast against the black material as they rose and fell with her breath.

"Maybe," she said with a laugh, "but you're also the most unselfish, most thoughtful person I've known in a long time."

Candlelight flickered over her face, adding a pulsing glow to her beauty. With her so temptingly close, he decided to ease up on his rule about keeping space between them. Lifting a lock of her hair from her breast, he brushed it against his lips. "You ought to do that more often."

"Do what?"

"Look at me that way."

She turned her soft smile toward the stage, giving him time to drink in her profile. Her thick honey-colored lashes, that pert nose, those glistening pink lips and that graceful column of her neck made him ache to pull her into his arms and taste her all over. But he knew he wouldn't, knew he couldn't until she gave him a clear signal that she was ready. Unfortunately, the way she was nibbling at her bottom lip again told him she wasn't about to wave the get-over-here-and-kiss-me flag just yet.

"Megan?"

Her guilty glance and the way she quickly lowered her lashes stung him in the heart. She reached for her drink and had it raised halfway to her lips before changing her mind and returning it to the purple cocktail napkin.

"Are you sure you're not expecting too much from me? I haven't been...well, around much. Nick, I'm as far from sophisticated as you can get."

"Hey, sweet girl," he said, lifting her chin on his fingers, "is that what you're worrying about? Because you've been reading me all—"

She pressed her cool, wet fingers against his lips, stopping him in midsentence.

"Wait. You have to understand. I've chosen to spend my life in a town that lives by train whistles and church bells and school-bus schedules. I'm not complaining, Nick, because I wouldn't have it any other way."

"I can't imagine you anywhere else, either," he said.

"That's just it, though. I haven't spent the last ten years moving around the country, like you, having...well, experiences. Nick, I'm twenty-eight years old and I've never..." She took her hand from his mouth, and turning away began nervously toying with her earring.

"Meggie, we're friends first. Whatever is on your mind," he said, gently turning her face back toward his, "just say it."

She opened her mouth, but instead of talking she held her breath.

"Breathe."

She let her words rush out on her exhalation. "I've never seen a striptease before."

He leaned back against the red leather banquette and laughed until his eyes were moist.

"It's not funny," she said, her flitting gaze telling him she was more embarrassed than annoyed with his response.

"Megan, you're not going to see one now, either."

"But that poster outside in the lobby is so suggestive."

"It does set a mood," he said with an agreeing nod. "But I have it from a good source that Indigo Malone is not going to flash us." When Megan's questioning expression remained, he added, "I was playing basketball over at the gym the other night. By the way, Rebecca's husband was playing, too." He stopped to laugh and shake his head. "The guy almost flunked me in history my senior year, but that's another story. Anyway, my electrical contractor was there, too, and he said he brought his wife here last week. He assured me the show is in good taste. Good fun. His wife loved it."

Megan gave him a totally bogus smile and he could feel the lighthearted evening taking on the weight of a bad decision. His. Maybe Megan's interest in sexy dance numbers was confined to her kitchen performances.

"Look, if you feel uncomfortable with this, we can leave before the show—" His sentence broke off as the room lights went down, a drumroll began and a spotlight circled the stage.

Megan was looking toward the nearest exit as one spotlight separated into four and began tumbling in a seemingly frantic search for the dancer. The curtain went up, drawing her attention back to the spots, which were merging into one huge circle of light to surround the scantily dressed Indigo Malone.

Nick's quick glance toward Megan turned into a guarded stare. Like everyone else in the audience her attention had instantly riveted to the shapely long-legged dancer in the French-cut indigo velvet costume. Megan's lip parted and her eyes widened as Indigo Malone began a series of moves that made the bugle beads fringing her hips glint and glimmer.

"We can slip out now and no one will notice,"

Nick whispered as he groped in his jacket for his wallet. The sooner he put this fiasco behind them the better. Pulling out a bill, he dropped it on the table, then started to slide out of the banquette.

"That's okay," she said, reaching for his wrist and tugging him back without taking her eyes from the stage. "I mean…as long as you paid…we, uh, might as well…you know, stay."

When the beautiful dancer with the feather-and-sequin mask maneuvered her hips in a provocative yet playful shimmy, Nick held his breath and waited for Megan's reaction. He was prepared for anything but what he saw. Megan propped her elbows on the table, leaned her chin into the cup she made with her hands and drank in every move.

Skillfully combining her sexy, sinuous style with occasional touches of humor, the dancer rode a fine line between naughty and risqué. Nick wished he could see more than Megan's widened eyes and arched brows, but she kept the lower part of her face covered with her fingers during the number. By the time Indigo Malone had taken a second curtain call, the audience was on its feet and applauding.

"We can beat the crowd, if we leave by that side door," he said. Her look of displeasure had him mildly confused. "What? You're not interested anymore in taking that walk on the beach that we planned during dinner?"

"Sure. But maybe she's coming back for another curtain call. We wouldn't want to miss anything."

"Miss anything?" he asked, shaking his head as he tried not to laugh. "By the way you were staring, I doubt if you missed a single shimmy during that performance.''

"How could anyone not watch her?'' Megan asked, opening her palms and spreading her arms before she went back to applauding. "She was wonderful.''

"So let me get this straight. You're saying I haven't corrupted you?'' he asked with a deadpan expression as he took her hand and led her through the crowd toward the side exit.

"Okay. I'll admit I was wrong,'' she said as they headed out the exit and across the boardwalk. "I absolutely loved it.''

He nodded, his deadpan expression still fixed on his face. "Good, because I'm giving a test later and I want to see you do that thing Indigo did with her hips when the drummer—ouch!''

"I should have known!'' she said, playfully smacking his arm again. "You still are the bad boy my mother warned me about.''

As they removed their shoes, her laughter lasered through the last of his misgivings like an unstoppable beam of energy directed at his heart. He peeled off his socks, and when they walked down the steps and onto the cool sand she began humming a slow and sexy number from the show.

Something special had happened to her while she was watching the exotic dancer. Something fun and liberating. He wasn't sure of the extent yet, or how long it would last. That it had happened at all was the important thing, because that meant it could happen again.

He smiled to himself. "Last one in the water walks

home,'' he said, heading toward the water in a dead run.

The sand gritting beneath his feet, the sound of her laughter mixing with the thundering waves and an unnameable happiness he'd never experienced before threw the moment into a surreal spectacle of the senses. She called his name and he turned to look back. The horde of humanity strolling the boardwalk, a huge flock of noisy seagulls suddenly taking flight and the garish neon light spilling over the scene only added to the high-spirited atmosphere. And right in the middle of the crazy panorama was a blond and laughing goddess running toward him.

Stopping dead in his tracks, he braced his hand against a lifeguard stand and watched her coming. He thought he'd never seen anything so beautiful. Each step she took closer to him had his heart pounding with joy and the rest of him aching with desire.

She arrived at his side, out of breath and shaking her head. ''What a surprising night this is turning out to be,'' she said, dropping her evening bag in the sand and pushing back her hair.

''What a surprising woman you're turning out to be. I think you were having as much fun watching Indigo Malone's dance as she was having performing it.''

''I think you're right,'' she said, still a little breathless. They stared at each other for a few seconds before they broke into grins.

''Nick, about that mask she wore. Why do you think she didn't take it off at the end? I mean, a lot of people in the audience were shouting for her to remove it.''

''Did you want her to remove it?'' He rested his

crooked elbow on the lifeguard chair and waited for her reply.

She looked at him for a long while, then slowly shook her head. "No. No, I didn't."

"Why?" he asked, genuinely intrigued with her careful consideration of the question.

Lacing her fingers behind her back, she took a few steps away from him and looked out over the moonlit water. Her unfocused stare continued until a warm land breeze blew up behind them. Smiling, she reached for the hem of her dress to hold it against her legs. The breeze continued, tossing her hair into a free-form halo around her head. As he watched the interplay of nature and her feminine maneuverings, he found himself tugging at his tie, gulping in air and forgetting that he was waiting for her answer. Then she turned to him and spoke.

"I think I've figured it out. Because as long as she keeps that mask on, she remains in control of both of her identities. She keeps the fantasy alive that way, too, and in the end, I think, no one is disappointed."

"Megan," he said, reaching out to urge her closer, "I'm sure there's deep meaning to that observation, but if I don't kiss you soon, I swear you'll have me howling at the moon."

Her laughing eyes dared him.

"I mean it," he teased. "They'll hear me up on the boardwalk."

Megan took three slow steps to where he stood, slipped her hands around the back of his neck and brought her lips a whisper away from his. "Howl away."

He pressed his lips to hers instead in a hot, deep,

demanding kiss. The effect shattered all of Megan's good intentions to keep him at a controllable distance from her heart.

They were together. On a deserted beach. Away from everything and everyone that filled her days and gave purpose to her life. There was no purpose in this moment, only an opportunity to start something she knew she shouldn't. No purpose at all. Only selfish need and plenty of it. Dammit, why shouldn't she enjoy Nick? What was the harm in a few kisses on a moonlit beach?

Megan sighed into the kiss, swirling her tongue inside his mouth and stroking it until his arms went around her in a full embrace. They could be spinning through space on the sunny side of Venus or the dark side of the moon. It didn't matter. They were somewhere in the heavens, holding each other so close she didn't know where he began or she ended. The next thing she knew he was lifting her and she was wrapping her legs around his hips. The kiss went on and on, sending surge after surge of pleasure through her body. He turned her around and broke the kiss as he sat her bottom in the crook of the chair supports. This time there was no teasing glint in his eyes, only a longing that reached inside and wrapped around her heart.

She whispered his name as she drew her fingers through his hair, then down his cheeks. He caught her thumb in his teeth and nipped gently at the fleshy pad, making her gasp with deep, sharp pleasure that promised more of the same.

"Meggie, you make me feel like I did that night ten

years ago. The night I left. I never wanted anyone so badly then or since.''

"I don't know what's happening to me," she said, feathering kisses across his forehead. "Ever since I saw that dancer, I feel as if I'm someone else.''

"It's called self-discovery, when you least expect it.''

"Is it? Or is this all make-believe? I don't know.'' She shook her head in growing confusion. She felt like a stranger in her own skin, yet she had never felt more real in her entire life.

He bowed his head to plant a kiss on one breast. The exquisitely slow skim of his open mouth on her skin made the empty space inside her quiver.

"What *do* you know?"

"That I never in a million years thought I'd feel like this," she whispered, staring into his eyes.

He bowed his head to kiss her other breast. "Like what?''

When he lifted his mouth, she stepped down onto the sand. His quiet questions loosened her tongue more effectively than any form of torture she could have imagined. "Like I've always wanted to feel. Nick, the way you're looking at me, the way you kiss me…''

Shaking her hands she took a step backward, then turned and began to pace a small strip of sand next to the chair. "Please try to understand. I just can't jump into this," she said, wondering if his patience was wearing thin and praying that it wasn't. "I need a little more time." Time to figure out how she was going to manage an affair without driving Nick crazy, without taking time away from Paige and without destroying her own heart in the process. There was a way. She simply had to figure it out.

"Maybe we should go now," she whispered as she picked up her evening bag and started back across the sand. She'd taken two steps when he snared her around the waist.

"I'll give you all the time you need, but I don't want us to lose this feeling." He pulled her against him in an embrace that left no doubt as to how much he wanted her. "I don't want to wake up tomorrow and find out that you've decided to pretend this night never happened. Tell me you won't do that."

"I could never pretend this didn't happen," she said, sinking back in his embrace. *Even when you leave Follett River and I have to pick up my life and go on without you.* "Never."

"That's all I wanted to hear," he said, holding her close for a few more seconds.

"Thank you," she whispered.

Letting go, he took her hand and headed with her toward the steps to the boardwalk. "Let's hope our shoes are still there. They frown on barefeet on the casino floors."

"We're not going home?" she asked, surprised that he still wanted to spend more time with her.

"Megan Sloan," he said, giving her his best lunatic frown as he waved toward the row of casinos lining the boardwalk for as far as the eye could see. "Where are you?"

"Atlantic City, but—"

"No buts. You're getting the grand tour tonight."

Her heart skipped a beat when she realized he meant

to take her gambling. Memories of her dead husband rushed in, threatening to pull her under in their wake.

Andy had brought her gambling a few times, but she quickly found she hated coming. More to the point, she hated seeing their hard-earned money disappear. She looked at Nick as he reached for their shoes. Calm down, she told herself. Nick wasn't Andy. Nick's money was his own, not theirs. He could do whatever he wished with it. It was of no concern to her, because she didn't have a future with Nick. Only the possibility of a short-term affair, if she decided to go through with it. Meanwhile, the rest of her life was her business and the rest of Nick's life was his.

"Have a seat, Cinderella," he said, breaking into her thoughts.

Smiling, she sat down on the step. Why hadn't she thought of it before? A night spent watching Nick gamble was the most logical thing that could happen at this point. Seeing him throw his hard-earned money around like confetti would put every errant, overly romanticized thought about them in proper perspective. True, Nick Buchanan was the most exciting and desirable man she'd ever known. He was also the first man to make her consider rearranging her life, if only for a few short months, to make him a part of it. But she wasn't about to fall in love with him. She'd decided years ago that she could never have a future with another irresponsible man. But having Nick as a lover was a completely different thing, she thought as he brushed sand from her foot, then gave it a teasing squeeze before he slipped on the first shoe.

Megan lifted her chin from her pillow, opened one eye and squinted with concentration toward her radio

# NO RISK, NO OBLIGATION TO BUY...NOW OR EVER!

# CASINO JUBILEE

## "Scratch 'n' Match" Game

### Here's how to play:

1. Peel off label from front cover. Place it in the space provided opposite. With a coin carefully scratch away the silver box. This makes you eligible to receive three or more free books, and possibly another gift, depending upon what is revealed beneath the scratch-off area.

2. Send back this card and you'll receive specially selected Silhouette® novels from the Desire™ series. These books are yours to keep absolutely FREE.

3. There's no catch. You're under no obligation to buy anything. We charge nothing for your first shipment. And you don't have to make any minimum number of purchases – not even one!

4. The fact is thousands of readers enjoy receiving books by mail from the Reader Service™, at least a month before they're available in the shops. They like the convenience of home delivery, and of course postage and packing is completely FREE!

5. We hope that after receiving your free books you'll want to remain a subscriber. But the choice is yours – to continue or cancel, any time at all! So why not take up our invitation, with no risk of any kind. You'll be glad you did!

**YOURS FREE!**

*You'll look a million dollars when you wear this lovely necklace! Its cobra-link chain is a generous 18" long, and the lustrous simulated pearl completes this attractive gift.*

ENLARGED TO SHOW DETAIL

# CASINO JUBILEE
## "Scratch 'n' Match" Game

SCRATCH HERE ?

PLACE LABEL HERE

## CHECK CLAIM CHART BELOW
## FOR YOUR FREE GIFTS!

D8HI

**YES!** I have placed my label from the front cover in the space provided above and scratched away the silver box. Please send me all the gifts for which I qualify. I understand that I am under no obligation to purchase any books, as explained on the back and on the opposite page. I am over 18 years of age.

MS/MRS/MISS/MR          INITIALS

BLOCK CAPITALS PLEASE

SURNAME

ADDRESS

POSTCODE

### CASINO JUBILEE CLAIM CHART

| | | | |
|---|---|---|---|
| 🍒 | 🍒 | 🍒 | WORTH 4 FREE BOOKS AND A FREE NECKLACE |
| 🍒 | 🔔 | 🍒 | WORTH 4 FREE BOOKS |
| 🍒 | BAR | 🍒 | WORTH 3 FREE BOOKS    CLAIM Nº 1,528 |

THE READER SERVICE™
FREEPOST SEA3794
CROYDON
Surrey
CR9 3AQ

alarm clock. Her sleep-fogged brain was telling her the clock read 7:13, but the noise that had jolted her awake was the 7:00 a.m. train whistle. Or was it? Come to think of it the noise was more of an intermittent yipping than the long blasts she was familiar with. Frowning, she managed one slow-motion shake of her head.

Figuring out that little mystery went straight to the bottom of her list of priorities when her sleepy-eyed stare wandered from the angular red numbers on the radio to the soft folds of her cocktail dress draped over a chair. As memories from last night rushed in, she felt her frown shifting and lifting into what she knew was an easy, silly smile. In the end Nick hadn't disappointed her. After ten minutes at the roulette wheel he took her hand and walked away, telling her she was much more interesting to look at.

"Nick," she whispered, remembering how he had run his fingertips over the satin spaghetti straps and onto her shoulders. How he'd smoothed his hands over the formfitting bodice in a way that made the tips of her breasts tighten with anticipation. Then, in one combustible moment, how he crushed the dress between their bodies as he lifted her into his arms and kissed her.

Whispering his name again, she closed her eyes and sighed as more wonderful scenes from last night came back to her. Each one caused subtle yet distinctly pleasurable sensations in the feminine recesses of her body. "Yes, yes, yes," she whispered, burying her face in her pillow. Whether she could afford him or

not, Nick Buchanan was the one luxury in her life she
had to have.

So what if the next few months were going to be
busier than usual? She would make it all work, she
told herself as she began to review the challenges facing her. She had a series of firmly scheduled appoint-
ments with Cranberry Real Estate and Rentals to view
several properties. Once she found a house suitable to
live in and run her catering business from, she had to
set up a meeting with the bank. Two of her waitresses
were thinking about quitting and she would have to
find replacements for them. By next week she would
be in the middle of making Jade Macleod's wedding
cake. Paige had two more fittings for her flower-girl
dress. And then there was Paige's first day of school.
She suddenly pictured the adoring gazes her daughter
had sent Nick's way, and she was reminded once again
that she had to be careful. Protecting her own heart
from being broken was something she would have to
manage, but Paige's was another matter. Tiny hearts
were fragile. If there was one thing she had to make
sure of, it was that Paige wouldn't suffer because of
her relationship with Nick.

Reaching for the dress, she rubbed the black silk
against her lips. Breathing in the scent of her perfume
and the trace of his aftershave, she thought about his
nearness and how that made her feel. With an elaborate groan, she rolled onto her back and stared up at
the ceiling.

"Ah, Nick," she murmured, "am I crazy to think
we can be together…be lovers for a little while…
without the rest of my life crumbling at my feet?"

If Nick meant what he'd said about giving her space and letting her lead the way, she just might be able to pull this off. She wouldn't ask much of him. Just a little of his time every now and then. His understanding about her situation. She nibbled at her lip as she tried and failed to suppress a smile. And to make good on that line in her high-school yearbook, by allowing her to surprise him with her secret fantasies.

As wild and deliciously erotic thoughts came to mind, she covered her face with the dress to muffle still another groan. Nick Buchanan was either going to be her escape route from her pressure cooker of a life or a detour straight into hell. Either way the time ahead was going to be memorable.

Dragging the dress from her face, she closed her eyes, and was in the middle of taking a deep breath when the strange yipping noise started again. Followed by Paige's hysterical laughter. Both of Megan's eyelids flew open.

"What in the world...?" Megan pushed off her bed and bounded for the living room, where she discovered Paige lying on her back on the floor. A small white puppy tugged at her hair.

"Mommy! Look!" she said, raising her head, and in the process, the puppy's front legs. "Santa Claus didn't forget me. He brought me my puppy."

The frisky ball of fur stopped its playful tugging and turned its curious eyes to Megan. Letting go of Paige's hair, the small dog dropped his paws to the floor, wagged its springy tail and walked over to Megan to sniff her toes.

"Whose puppy is this?" she asked, looking around the room as the small dog began licking her toes.

"Mommy," Paige said in an exasperated tone. "I told you. He's mine. Come here, Beans." She patted her small hands on the carpet and the dog came running. "See? He knows his name is Beans."

"Yes, I see," Megan said as she ran her fingers through her hair again. This time she held on to a lock and spoke slowly. "But where did this puppy come from?"

"From in that basket with all these doggie toys and stuff," she said, holding up a jingling toy before pointing to a wicker basket with a huge red bow tied to its handle.

"Beans was outside on the porch. And—" She looked up at her mother. "I know I'm not supposed to answer the door before you say so, but Beans was crying."

A dull, throbbing ache started at her temples. She let go of her hair and began rubbing the sides of her head. "It's okay. I'm not mad at you, sweetheart. I just want to know who brought you the puppy," she said, hoping against hope that her first suspicion was wrong.

"Santa brought him. Isn't he 'dorable?" Paige asked between giggles. "I knew Santa wouldn't forget me. He wrote me a letter. Look. It's in the basket. I read my name on it. You read the inside, Mommy. I want to know what Santa says to me."

Megan sat down on the sofa and wearily reached into the basket. Glancing at Paige's name written across the folded note, Megan recognized the handwriting. But then she knew she would. Blinking back tears of frustration, she dropped the note into her lap without bothering to unfold it.

"Read it to me."

Pain and joy lumped together in her throat and she had to swallow twice before she could continue. "Santa says you were a very good girl. You're one of his favorites, but..." she began without looking at the note. She pressed her fingers to the bridge of her nose and waited for two tears to disappear. "Paige," she said softly. "Paige, Santa made a mistake."

"Oh, no, he didn't. Beans is just the right size. And see his tongue? It's pink!"

"Paige, I need you to come here and sit beside me. We have to talk."

"Okay." The little girl stood, yanked up on the waistband of her footie pajamas, then scooped up the puppy. "But first you have to hold Beans," she said, dropping him in Megan's lap. "Here, Mommy. Hold him like this, so he can kiss you."

Megan closed her eyes as the squirming puppy pressed its paws against her breast and stretched to lick her. One day, when she'd rented that house with a fenced-in yard and when her work schedule became more manageable, Paige would have her puppy. Right now, with no one at home during the day, there was no way they could keep this one. Chewed woodwork, constant barking and those inevitable accidents would not be tolerated by an already difficult-to-deal-with landlord. She squeezed back tears when the thought came to mind that even if those obstacles could be dealt with, she didn't have the money for an extra security deposit.

"He tickles more when he kisses your cheek," Paige said as she moved a lock of her mother's hair behind her ear.

"Oh, Mommy, I can't wait to show Heather," she said, patting Megan's knees. "Heather said Santa forgot me. But he didn't forget me, because I was so good. Just like Santa said. Wasn't I, Mommy? Mommy, why are you crying?"

"Sweetheart, I'm not crying," she said, swiping her knuckles under her eyes as she made a hasty, if not downright cowardly decision to put off explaining to Paige that the puppy had to go.

*And so did Nick Buchanan.*

He belonged in her fantasies, not in her life. Not anywhere *near* her life. She'd been temporarily insane to consider inviting him closer. The next time she saw Nick Buchanan she was going to wring his neck, she decided as she carefully set the wiggling puppy onto the floor. And that next time was going to be soon.

"Why don't we get dressed and take Beans for a little walk? Then we can take him downstairs to the kitchen to show him to Nancy and Connie while we wait for Aunt Sandra to pick you up."

*And we'll all say a prayer that this morning isn't the morning for a surprise visit from the health inspector while I'm off paying a visit to ol' St. Nick himself!*

# Six

"Hold on! I'll be right there."

In the short time it took Nick to wrap a towel around his waist, yank open the bathroom door and make a wet trail of footprints across the suite's plush carpeting, the knocking on his door had turned into a series of loud bangs. He cast his glance toward the ceiling. This was Saturday morning, dammit! Who the hell…? Groaning, he pictured his second-in-command, Rocky Nolan, standing in the hall.

Frowning, Nick plowed his fingers through his wet hair, then wiped his hands on his terry-cloth covered hips. Rocky Nolan was better than competent, he was good enough to run the operation. If there was an area of Rocky's work that needed attention, it was his serious lack of self-confidence.

Nick pinched the bridge of his nose and took a

104    TALL, DARK AND TEMPORARY

calming breath. Hopefully, all Nolan needed was a pep talk. Adjusting the towel, Nick glanced at the clock on the desk and thought about his plans for his day off. A very short pep talk.

He focused on leveling a reasonable but serious look at the person on the other side, then reached for the doorknob. "Rocky, my man, you—" When he saw the person on the other side, Nick took a step forward and grinned. "Shaved off that mustache."

"Take another look," Megan said, leaning back to steal a glance down the hall. In the distance, Nick could hear a soft bell signaling the arrival of one of the elevators. "This isn't Rocky."

Shoving her hands against Nick's wet chest hair, Megan pushed him back into the room. Before he could speak, she snatched the Do Not Disturb sign from the inside of the door and hooked it over the outside knob. Closing the door with a solid slam, she whirled around to face him.

"Just what the hell were you thinking of?"

Nick looked at her for a long moment, then sighed. "And this would be about the puppy."

"Of course, this would be about the puppy," she said, emphasizing each word with the heel of her hand against his chest.

"Bad move?" he asked, squinting at her as the first tickle of self-doubt started up the back of his neck.

"How could you have been so thoughtless? So insensitive to our situation? My little girl is about to have her heart broken because of this…this totally irresponsible action of yours. Of all the…" Her voice began trailing off as her steely stare dropped to his chest. She wiped her hand on her apron as her eyes widened and her lips parted. A few seconds later she looked away, gesturing wildly with both hands. "Geez, Nick, could you put some clothes on?"

Before he could reply, she headed over to the balcony doors. Grabbing the edge of the gold-fringed drapes, she pulled them closed, then snapped on a lamp.

"I was about to get dressed, when I—"

She looked back at him and then away. "Then do it!"

Nick started to cross the room toward the wardrobe. Halfway there, he stopped and turned back to her. He jutted his chin in her direction. "Don't you think 'thoughtless, insensitive and irresponsible' are pretty strong indictments just for giving Paige a puppy?"

"Strong or not, they don't make it any less true," she said heatedly. "What possessed you to do such a thing?"

"Not what, Megan. Who," he said, suddenly feeling a wave of righteous indignation over her response to his well-meant act. "Your daughter. She sat on my lap with tears in her eyes and whispered to me, with quivering lips I might add, that Santa promised her a puppy last Christmas. And because he didn't deliver, she's convinced she's been a bad little girl." As memories from his own childhood began working their way into his consciousness, he shook his head to rid himself of those images. "What was I supposed to do?" he asked, bouncing ten fingertips against his chest. "Just dip my heart in cement and forget what she said?"

"It's not that simple, Nick. Her happiness is my

responsibility. My business. You had no right to do this. You should have talked with me first.''

"I did," he said, his voice rising as he jammed his hands to his hips, "but you seem to have conveniently forgotten that conversation.''

"I guess I have," she said, brushing her hair from her forehead before jamming her hands to her hips in a parody of his own stance. "Why don't you refresh my memory?''

"Last week, out at the trailer. Remember? It was another one of those times you were trying to avoid talking about us...you do that all the time. You said you were planning on getting her a puppy. Soon.''

"I was. I am. But not this soon," she said, raising her hands and balling them into fists to stress her point. Her green-eyed gaze dropped to his chest again, lingering there for several seconds until she turned and began to pace.

Nick could tell by her rigid posture and strained voice that arguing with her was getting him nowhere. He started to think that there was more going on than anger over his surprise gift to her daughter. What exactly, he wasn't sure.

Maybe she thought engaging him in a heated argument would convince him to back off. Or was this morning's passionate display Megan's last-ditch effort to convince *herself* not to become his lover? He thought back to last night in Atlantic City, when she finally started to open up to him. She offered him a glimpse of who she could be. Of who she wanted to be. He would never forget those high-spirited moments on the beach, when she'd made his blood simmer and his heart melt. And just as important, he wasn't going to let her forget them, either.

Nick rubbed his face to hide his smile. *All this wasted effort, sweet girl,* he thought, *and I'm still wanting what I never had. You.*

"Ah, Meggie, loosen up," he said gently. "So Paige got her puppy sooner rather than later. What's the problem?"

When she didn't answer he walked back over to her. The instant he placed his hands around her arms, he could feel the tension in her body tightening. And he knew he had his work cut out for him. "You've got to start talking to me," he said evenly.

"You didn't ask me. Nick, I can't have you barging into my life and upsetting it with these grand gestures."

"It's just a puppy," he said as he ran his hands up and down her arms to soothe her. When he tried to urge her closer, she held her ground. "I meant it in the best possible way, but, Megan, what's done is done."

"For you, maybe," she said, breaking his hold as she stepped back from him. "But not for me. I have to be the bad guy now and tell her she can't keep it."

"What?" he asked, narrowing his eyes in confusion. "Why?"

"Nick, what am I going to do with it while I'm at work? This puppy, in case you didn't know, is not quite housebroken. I can't leave it in the apartment. I can't keep running upstairs all day long to take it out every hour, either."

"I agree. Didn't you read the note I put in the basket with it?"

She dismissed his question with a wave of her hand. "I didn't have to read the note. I knew it was from you."

"If you'd read it, you also would have known that daytime isn't going to be a problem. I'm planning to keep the dog in a run out at River Walk during work hours. I'll drop him off at your place afterward, and that way Paige can have him for the evening. By the time the project is complete the dog will be housebroken. See? This isn't as disastrous as you thought."

"I'm sorry, Nick. I just can't keep the dog," she said, attempting to sidestep him as she headed for the door.

He beat her there, slamming his hand against it before she could reach it. "Why?" His simple one-word question commanded her to answer. She hesitated. "What's going on, Megan?"

"All right!" she shouted as she shoved her fingers through her hair. "I can't afford a pet. There. Are you satisfied? Can I go now?"

Prickles slid down his spine. This was the last thing he expected to hear, yet he knew she wasn't lying. Not with that much emotion behind her delivery. "No," he said with one slow shake of his head.

"You're really not going to let me out of here until I tell you. Right?"

Folding his arms across his chest, he nodded. "Oh, yeah."

She pressed her fingers to her forehead and sighed. "My landlord just socked me with rent increases on both the apartment and the café. I knew it was coming, but I didn't expect it until after the first of the year. On top of that little surprise, I would have to come up with an extra security deposit for keeping a pet. That's another month's rent that I don't have.''

"What about your savings? Your investments?"

She gave him an incredulous look. "What are you talking about?"

"Surely Andy left you with some kind of capital. His insurance or—"

"Andy left us with nothing." She lowered her hands. "That's right, Nick. Nothing. When I told you he was coming home from a business trip the night he died…well, that wasn't exactly the truth. He'd been in Atlantic City gambling.''

For the sake of her embarrassment, Nick forced himself not to give in any further to the shock he was experiencing. He nodded understandingly. "I see.''

"No, you don't," she said, staring over his shoulder. "Nobody else would, either, if they knew." She rubbed at the space between her brows. "I've made a point of keeping quiet about his gambling problem, because I don't want Paige to have to hear bad things about her father." Her voice was still crackling with tension. "And I don't relish the thought of people's pitying stares, either." She looked up at him. "Nick, no one knows about this.''

He thought back to his own embarrassing circumstances during his childhood. He knew about pride, and how fragile a thing it was. "And no one will, Megan, but—"

"I'm doing the best I can. It's *not* always going to be this way," she said in a voice meant to squelch his possible skepticism. "I'm pinching every dime, trying to pull enough money together to go into full-time catering with Piece of Cake. Every dime, Nick.''

Grabbing the top of her apron, she pointed to where the straps attached to the front. "Take a good look. These aren't examples of abstract embroidery. They're tears I've had to mend because I can't afford a new apron. So tell me, Nick, if I can't afford that minor expense, how can I afford a puppy?"

Her shaking hands and quivering chin told him that admitting her precarious financial situation had nearly done her in. His first impulse was to pull her into his embrace and tell her he'd fix everything. He hesitated, pursing his lips in thoughtful consideration. From the way she'd reacted when he'd given her daughter a puppy, he knew he had to move carefully or risk losing her altogether. Her pride was on the line; offering to wipe out all her financial problems would guarantee irreversible damage to their relationship.

"Okay," he said in a reasoning voice. "First things first. You're right. I apologize for overstepping my bounds, but we're not going to break Paige's heart because of my mistake."

She eyed him suspiciously. "Really?" she asked, her voice a mixture of wariness and doubt. "And just how are we going to manage that?"

"We are going to allow me to pay the security deposit." He held up his hand when she started to protest. "Don't go there. I screwed up, not you."

"I didn't come here for a handout."

"Tell me something I don't already know. Like why you haven't mentioned your plans to me before now about going big time with Piece of Cake? All these weeks we've spent together and you've never once let on." He lifted her chin on his crooked fingers and looked into her eyes. "What's happened to you? Ten years ago you didn't have a problem communicating your hopes and dreams to me.''

"That was a few lifetimes ago." She strained to bring herself under control, but the edge of bitterness in her voice had already reached his ears. "Besides, my business plans are no concern of yours."

"Look," he said softly, "I'm not kidding myself. I know we don't have much of a shared history, but in that short time we spent together back then, we connected."

"Back then..." Shaking her head, she walked away. "Nick, I'm not a naive teenager anymore. Things have happened."

"What things?"

"Life. Ten years of life. I've come down from the clouds and learned to be realistic."

"Go on. Realistic about what?"

"I'm not interested in being married to a district attorney or living in a big house out on Red Oak Road anymore. I just want to work at something I like, pay my bills and be a good mother to Paige. That's all."

Megan was just about everything he'd remembered her to be. A good and loving person. Honorable, responsible, determined, and once again, standing at a crossroads in her life. And she was still so damn beautiful she made him ache. He didn't doubt for a second that she could and would realize her goals, but something about Megan *had* changed. Something he could feel, though he couldn't yet put it into words.

Moving beside her, he took in the determined tilt of her chin, her steady if not quite focused stare and the way she was trying for slow, deep breaths and failing. One more step brought him in front of her. Her eyes glistened as he slowly ran his fingers through her hair, then tucked it behind her ears. "Megan?" he said softly.

She shook her head, refusing to meet his gaze. He said her name again, and as if a lingering fog suddenly lifted from the horizon, the answer came to him in a burst of pure light. The golden girl of his youth had been scarred by life more deeply than he could have imagined. Megan still had plans, but she'd given up on dreams. Sobered by the knowledge, he looked away.

It was one thing to pursue an available and desirable woman. But was he being selfish to still want an intimate relationship with her, knowing what he did now? The last thing he wanted to do was add confusion to her hectic life. Maybe the best thing he could do for her would be to back off altogether. Well, not altogether. Maybe an uncomplicated friendship was what she needed most. Maybe.

He looked back at her in time to see two shimmering tears forming in the corners of her eyes.

Two tears she desperately didn't want him to see.

Two tears that washed away his doubt and opened a floodgate of new emotion when they slipped onto her cheeks and she blotted them away with a corner of her apron.

There were no maybes left after that, only the intolerable feeling that he could lose her if he made the wrong move or said the wrong thing. As he continued to look at her, he realized there was only one thing to do. To keep telling her the truth until she believed him.

He touched his fingertips to her face and raised it

to his. "I meant no harm with the puppy. I mean no harm with this."

"With what?" she whispered, searching his eyes with her tear-brightened ones.

"This," he said, bringing his mouth to hers for a slow and soulful kiss. From her trembling lips and ragged breath, he sensed she was fighting her natural desire to respond. The inner strength that had always served her well was now her greatest enemy. And his.

"Megan," he whispered, playing his lips against hers. "Megan, let it go." Slipping his fingers down her neck, he deepened the dancing kiss with a gentle thrust of his tongue. Just when he thought she'd never touch him, she skimmed his rib cage with her fingertips. It was as if she'd gifted the light strokes to his manhood. Stepping forward he pressed his hips and the hard evidence of his arousal against her. She couldn't swallow her gasp fast enough.

He lifted his mouth from hers in time to see her eyes closing. They fluttered open a second later.

"Nick, we shouldn't start anyth—"

"We already have," he said, cutting her off in a quietly insistent tone. "Kiss me."

Megan kissed him. Quickly. Dutifully. And with a painful sigh she didn't try to hide. "There," she said, forcing herself not to lick the taste of him from her lips. "Are you satisfied?"

"That was awful," he said, shaking his head.

Her nerve endings were raw. Her breath was burning in her chest. *Of course, that was awful.* But it was the only way, if she was getting out of there anytime soon. She lowered her gaze.

"Don't criticize that kiss, Nick," she said, fighting

the almost overwhelming urge to press her mouth to his chest and tear off his towel. "It's the last one you're ever going to get from me."

She started to push away, but he snatched her back against him with a force that made her aware of every vital inch of him.

"Is it, Megan?" he asked, closing his hands over the small of her back and holding her hard against the unyielding length of him.

"Nick," she pleaded, but for what she wasn't sure. Relief? Continuation? Anything she wanted? Anything *he* wanted? Oh, yes, she thought, drawing her fingers against his hot, naked skin, through his crisp, dark chest hair, over the pebbly perfection of his nipples. Beneath it all, his pounding heart was sending an unrelenting message to every inch of her feminine flesh. This was temptation as she'd never known it. Yet always wished it to be. Nick was hers for the taking, but she'd taken so little in her life. And when she had, she'd paid dearly. What, she wondered, was the price of this? *Too much,* a voice inside her screamed. She raised her hands to his shoulders, meaning to push him away. The masculine feel of his broad, muscled shoulders beneath her small hands made the empty space inside her ache. She'd never felt anything quite so wonderful. Except maybe the way he was nuzzling his mouth against that spot right below her ear.

"Kiss me, Megan," he said, lifting his mouth as he slid his hands over her buttocks. "Kiss me like this is the beginning of something wonderful."

"Nick," she whispered in a protesting tone even she wasn't buying anymore.

He pulled back, smiling that smile that was more effective than truth serum. "'Nick,' what?"

No matter the outcome, she had to say it. Had to tell him in her own words what he must know already. What she had known from the beginning. "I'm afraid I won't stop."

"Who says I'd want you to?" he asked as his hungry gaze drifted over her body then back to her face.

"But—"

He gave her his best bad-boy smile. "Shut up and kiss me."

With a moan of surrender, she cupped a hand behind his head and pulled him close. Slanting her lips over his, she worked her mouth on his while her heart leapt around inside her chest like a bird trying out its wings for the first time.

And like a happy martyr to her sudden wantonness, Nick let her claim the kiss as her own, accepting her nibbles, her nudges, her outrageous licks with verbal encouragements that made her ears burn. Greedy for a deeper taste of him, she slid her tongue past the cinnamon taste of mouthwash clinging to his lips and began exploring the moist warmth beyond. She continued the bold, intimate act until he slipped his hand between them and drew it across her belly. Backing off to give him room, she looked down as he reached for the front slipknot on her apron. One tug on the string and in a matter of seconds he was slipping it off and dropping it over the chair. Looking into her eyes, he undid the buttons on her blouse and then the front catch on her bra.

"I thought about doing this so many times," he said, peeling off the clothing he'd undone and tossing it onto the chair. As he brushed the backs of his fingers against her nipples, the tips tightened beneath his touch.

"I thought about you doing this, too." She swallowed as pleasure threatened to bring her to her knees. "I've thought about it…a lot."

"I know."

"You do?"

"I've always known."

"You've always known what?"

"That there's a wildly sensual woman in there. And I want so much to meet the rest of her." Giving her another bad-boy smile, he leaned down to tease her nipple with his tongue.

*Did he know?* she thought as she ran her fingers through his thick, dark hair. *Did Nick know about her secret fantasies?* Everyone else thought that line in the yearbook was a joke. What had she done that would make Nick think differently? His name formed on her lips, but before she could ask her question, he flicked his tongue over the sensitive flesh at the tip of her breast and began to suckle it. Her question dissolved on her lips as she choked out his name. "Nick. Oh, Nick," she managed as he continued the deliciously wicked act of possession that told her more about the man than she ever imagined.

He stopped the tender torture to look up, but for the life of her, Megan couldn't recall what she wanted to ask him.

"You're holding your breath," he said as he kneeled before her. Her exhalation turned into a rush of laughter. "That's better. For a second there, I thought you weren't enjoying this."

Unzipping her skirt, he eased it down her hips. She stepped out of it and was toeing off her shoes when he reached for the waistband of her panty hose. The usually awkward maneuver turned into an erotic act of seduction when he began trailing kisses down her thighs. Such little kisses for so much unrelenting pleasure. She took a firm grip on his shoulders as her knees began to give.

"Hang in there, sweet girl. We're not quite through here." He peeled the panty hose from one foot and then the other before dropping them atop the pile of clothing.

They looked at each other with an intensity that shifted their world into slow-motion anticipation. Seconds ticked by before he curved his hands around the tops of her thighs. Leaning forward, he took one side of her panties between his teeth and drew the clingy material down her hip. She sank her fingers in his hair as the touch of his hot breath and moist tongue promised more pleasures to follow.

"What else have you been thinking about…a lot?" he asked as he stripped off her panties, then lazily drew his fingers across the nest of golden curls he'd uncovered.

Too moved from his delicate touch to speak, she left his hair in wild disarray to stroke her thumb across his bottom lip.

"Megan," he whispered, opening her hand and planting a supplicant's kiss in its palm. Unbearable pleasure was spreading through her hot and hungry body like forked lightning as he stood and said the words that set their world in motion. "For a little while?"

"Yes," she whispered, understanding that he meant his time in Follett River would be, unlike hers, counted on a few calendar pages. "Nick, I don't need forever. I just need."

"You make me crazy when you look at me like that," he said, lifting her up in his arms and taking her through the open French doors and into the bedroom of his suite. She didn't stop looking at him, touching him, kissing him until he placed her on his rumpled sheets.

Nick marveled at the miracle that had shown up at his door this morning. He couldn't get enough of her golden beauty, her nicely naughty tan line or the feeling that his life was about to change.

"What's wrong? Why are you waiting?"

Swearing in reaction to his almost painful arousal, he gave her a look that was part warning, part apology. "I pictured things going a little slower than this," he said, reaching into the nightstand for a handful of condoms he'd put there over a week ago.

"I didn't," she said, loosening his towel but holding it in place. "At least, not the first time."

She let go of the towel, but he caught it before it slipped completely off him. In a saner part of his brain he knew there was merit in slowing things down. He'd wanted to enter her slowly, to watch for her slightest response, read every sign and revel in every sweet inch of her. And he certainly meant to but when she stretched out her arms to him as she lay back on the pillows, his plans began to change. Dropping the towel, he tore open one of the packets and rolled on protection. Her next words shattered the rest of his resolve.

"Nick, please. Don't make me beg."

"Why not?" he asked, parting her thighs and filling her with an urgency that scared the hell out of him. "I would for you."

# Seven

**B**ecause she was warm, wet and perfectly giving to his passionate advance, Nick knew Megan was physically ready for him. Holding himself still inside her, he lingered in heavenly limbo. Breathing in the vanilla scent of her hair, he waited for a sign to continue. When she didn't give him one, he raised his head to look at her. She wouldn't meet his eyes. Her slightly parted lips and shocked expression confirmed what his sinking heart was telling him—he'd moved too quickly and would have to back off.

"We'll go slower," he said as he began withdrawing from her. An inch before his unwanted freedom, she clasped her hands around his hips and held him fast.

"No."

No? The word had never sounded so promising, but

he understood that her response was most likely a confused or embarrassed reaction to his bold move. "It's
okay," he said gently as he moved back a fraction of
an inch more. "I didn't mean to startle—"

"But I don't want you to stop," she whispered
fiercely as she dug her fingers into his flesh with a
lack of subtlety that made him ache to fill her again.

The temptation to return to her deep velvety center
was close to overwhelming, but until he was certain
she meant it he had to hold back. "Megan, are you
sure?" he asked, even as she tangled her legs with his.
"We could—"

"I'm sure," she said as she tightened her already
snug fit around the tip of his manhood. The startling
intensity of her intimate caress caused Nick to groan
loud and hard.

If her fervent words and beguiling move weren't all
the persuasion he needed, the way she was now staring
into his eyes turned the tide. Gone was his hesitant
lover, replaced with a sensual woman who knew what
she wanted. Him. Reveling in the emotional moment,
he managed a shaky smile. "How sure?"

She smiled back. "Very, very sure," she said, con-
tracting around him again.

"Megan," he said, moving ever so slowly back into
her, "you're one sweet surprise after another."

As her passionate nature continued to unfold with
breathy moans and long, wet kisses, Nick silently pro-
claimed himself the luckiest man on the planet.

"Nick, tell me I'm not imagining this…this—"

"I can promise you that," he said, stroking her
faster. She lifted her hips and took him deeper. "This
is as real as it gets."

Somehow they'd passed that graceless stage new lovers bravely suffered and gone straight to the place where intimate knowledge of each other's deepest desires ruled. When her soft sounds turned to desperate cries, he welcomed them as treasured torments to his tortured control. Every luscious bit of her was responding to him, as if they'd planned each quiver, each move and each profound sensation. He loved the way her body danced beneath him at the edge of total ecstasy. Loved it until he thought he'd go mad. He kissed her eyelids, her cheeks, her mouth. "I want all of you."

As if she were waiting for permission, Megan shifted beneath him and heaven began exploding in his arms. He'd never seen anything so powerfully beautiful as the exquisite expression playing across her face or heard anything so moving as the sound of her cry at her climax. The moment became part of him and he knew he would carry it with him forever. Happily surrendering his crumbling control, Nick joined her at the pinnacle of her release.

When the surging waves of pleasure finally subsided, Megan kept on touching him. Even after he'd withdrawn from her body and levered himself to her side, she kept her palm pressed against his chest. She couldn't remember ever feeling this wonderful. This adored. This whole. Her sensuous sigh turned into a throaty moan of pure delight when their wandering gazes caught and held. He laughed softly and the moment resonated with delicious uncertainty. "Nick?" She rolled toward him onto her stomach.

"I'll be right back," he said, kissing the curve of

her backside before pushing off the bed and heading for the bathroom.

Somewhere in the back of her mind she knew she ought to be throwing on her clothes and rushing out of there, but when he looked back, winked and shook his head, all she wanted was to welcome him back to the bed. Besides, with Paige and the puppy now at Aunt Sandra's and Nancy and Connie taking care of the café, she had no compelling reason to go.

Hugging the pillow, she closed her eyes and thought about their extraordinary lovemaking. No longer could she tell herself, nor did she want to, that the real Nick Buchanan wouldn't be as fabulous a lover as the fantasy Nick Buchanan. He was better than fabulous. Tender, patient, funny and deliciously wicked, he was everything a real lover should be.

A few minutes later she felt the mattress give with his weight. A second after that her skin tingled as he made a trail of kisses across her shoulders.

"Meggie, Meggie, Meggie," he whispered, each time taking her name to another level of reverence. "You take my breath away."

She opened her eyes to watch him watching her. His loving gaze filled her with a new kind of longing. A yearning so intense, she couldn't find a word for it. Tears of joy tickled her eyes. She touched his face and tried to speak.

"What is it, sweet girl?"

She had to swallow twice before she managed to whisper, "I can't stop wanting you."

He nodded. "I know that feeling."

"Can we…?"

He was reaching for another condom and accidentally knocking his pager off the nightstand before she finished. Ignoring the thunking sound as the pager hit the rug, Nick ripped open the packet and quickly rolled on the contents.

He reached for her and was hard inside her in an instant. The world was spinning out of control again, but this time she knew where they were going—to that dark and thundering place beyond mere bliss.

Afterward as they shared the same pillow, he planted soft kisses on her brow. "So where do we go from here?"

She stopped drawing imaginary ovals around his navel and took a deep breath. "We have to consider how this will impact our lives."

Her choice of words made him smile. He had a feeling that their love nest had just changed into a war room. "Oh, absolutely," he said, wondering what strategy she was concocting.

"I mean, because we both have very busy lives outside of...this."

"This. Right," he said, concentrating on the silky feel of her hair as he looped a lock of it around his fingers. That she was attempting to sound sophisticated and worldly touched him. But she needn't have; he was more than happy to have the natural woman.

"I don't know about you, but I've *got* to keep on track with my life. Right now, I've got so much going on with my work. All of it's going to have a direct bearing on my future."

"Uh, yeah. Me, too," he said, thinking about the promotion he hoped was coming his way soon. A promotion that would place him in a position he'd been wanting for six years. Reaching over the edge of the bed, he picked up his pager and replaced it on the nightstand. He turned back to her and cringed inwardly when he saw worry lines where only minutes ago there had been frenzied signs of pagan pleasure. Cupping her chin in his hand, he tried to reassure her with a soft kiss. "Megan, we'll be okay with this."

"Of course. It's just going to take a little planning."

He quirked a brow as he lowered his hand from her chin. "Planning? We're not designing a military campaign."

"That's not what I meant. Nick, Follett River is a small town. People talk."

Rubbing the back of his neck, he finally nodded. "I know. I used to live here," he said, remembering the cruel remarks some people had whispered during his poverty-stricken childhood. Nevertheless, he'd lived through that and the later years when, because of his rebellious teens, he'd probably deserved some of those comments. His life was different now. The pain was an unpleasant memory, nothing more. And these past few weeks in Follett River had done much to lay those old ghosts to rest. "But, Megan, we're adults."

"Thank you for reminding me," she said, giving him a teasing smile. "In fact, I haven't felt so adult in a long, long time." She let her bold gaze ride the length of him before looking away with a sigh.

"What is it?"

"Nick, I'm also Paige's mother. I don't want her to have to deal with...well, it only takes a few unkind remarks to shatter a child's world. And kids can be especially cruel."

"Trust me," he said, taking her in his arms. "No

one's going to have a reason to gossip. The last thing I'd ever want is to see that little girl hurting.''

Nick was true to his word. Each morning he stopped by Megan's apartment, he stayed only long enough to pick up Beans. During Megan's daily deliveries at the job site, Nick kept his distance, never saying or doing anything to arouse his workers' curiosity. And though his visits to the café increased, he spent more time getting reacquainted with his old friends, calling in reports on his cell phone to the Murano Group's home office or finding new ways to sneak secret looks at Megan. Self-discipline took on new meaning when he found his steadfast adherence to discretion turning into an elaborate game that only served to tighten the sexual tension between them. He never complained; their time together was all that more exciting because of it.

On their planned nights together, he would wait inside the locked west entrance to the Hotel Maxwell to let her in. Two weeks into their relationship she was almost spotted by two of her regular café customers as she walked across the parking lot. Nick managed to whisk her inside the building and then into the stairwell without them being seen.

''That was close,'' she whispered, slamming her hands to her chest as she tried to catch her breath. Pale blond streamers of hair danced around her face as she leaned against the door. A rich pink colored her cheeks and her eyes sparkled with excitement as she shook her head. ''I should have come my usual way, but I was running late and I thought maybe you'd think I wasn't coming.''

A slow tickle started up the back of his neck. Didn't

she trust him to be there for her? Didn't she know he would have waited? Didn't she know how much she'd come to mean to him? "Did you think I'd leave you waiting out there?"

She took one more deep, calming breath and laughed as she glanced behind her. "I guess I wasn't thinking straight. I had a lot of things on my mind today. Paige left tonight with Andy's parents for that week at their beach house. They promised they'd pick her up at seven, but they were late..." Megan shrugged. "Whatever," she added, as she turned toward the door. Standing on her tiptoes, she looked through the tiny, chicken-wired window into the hallway.

Nick studied her in the harsh light spilling in from the hall. His heart thumped against his rib cage. Time and trouble hadn't tampered with her beauty. But the added stress of their clandestine relationship had her tap-dancing on a razor's edge. "Are you sure you're handling all this okay?"

"It works for me," she said as she twisted her neck to look up the hallway. "How about you?"

"Megan, this is crazy."

"What's crazy?" she whispered, ducking quickly as someone walked by the door.

"This!" he hissed as he flattened himself against the wall. "We're acting like you're my backstreet mistress. Like we're having a tawdry little affair, and it's not like that. It's become much—" He stopped talking the second he saw her shoulders drop and freeze. "Uh, Megan?"

She slowly turned around to face him, her eyes widening. "What did you say?" she asked as she crossed her arms beneath her breasts.

He hurriedly raised his palms in a placating gesture. "Sorry. That was a really bad choice of words. You're not anything like that."

"Really?" she asked, her deadpan expression revealing nothing to help him gauge the extent of the damage he'd done.

"I mean, it's not as if we're two repressed Victorians hurrying off to a shadowy tryst." Her brows lifted, but her eyes never left his as she turned her face a fraction of an inch away from him. "What? What's that look for?"

She took a step closer. "Why, Nick Buchanan, you naughty boy," she whispered, pushing him firmly against the wall next to the fire hose. Biting back a slow and wicked smile, she reached to draw her hands down his chest, then hook her fingers over his belt. Her sparkling green eyes were positively electric with interest. "You say the most...stimulating things," she said, allowing her thumbs to stray over his fly.

His gaze shifted from side to side before looking down at her. It seemed to him that the more intimate their relationship became, the less she wanted to talk about any other part of their lives. The thought had been niggling at him for days, but right now it was not what was holding his attention.

He narrowed his gaze. "I do?"

"Oh, yes," she said, reaching to place one hand high up on the inside of his thigh. Nibbling at his ear, she asked, "Just how tawdry is this affair you're having with your mistress?"

"*My* mistress?"

When she pinned him to the cinder-block wall with a slow, hot kiss, a growing spark of suspicion suddenly flamed to total comprehension. She was blatantly inviting him to engage in a game of erotic playacting. That she trusted him enough to make such a daring request excited him beyond all reason.

"Shamelessly tawdry," he said, undoing the buttons of her ivory colored knit top. Tugging down the demicups of her lacy bra, he palmed the dusky tips of her breasts until they quivered with stiffening resistance. He lowered his head to plant kisses on each satiny curve. "I find I'm wanting her all the time."

"All the time," she murmured in agreement.

He reached beneath the short navy blue skirt she wore and slid a slow hand up her thigh. "I can't wait to get my hands on her so I can do this," he whispered against her ear as he nudged aside the crotch of her panties and slipped a finger into her wetness.

Megan moaned. "Night and day?"

"It doesn't matter anymore," he said, stirring deeper into her velvety hot center. "But I wonder...does it matter to her?"

"Yes...I mean, no. It doesn't matter. Anytime he wants her, she's ready for him." She stopped to lick her lips. "Does he know that?"

He inserted a second finger and stroked her until she tightened around it. "He does now," he said, guiding her with his other hand until he'd pressed her into a shadowy corner of the stairwell. "Meggie, do you have any idea how close I am to lifting you up and taking you against this wall?"

She looked up through her thick-lashed half-closed

lids as she reached to stroke the hard length pressing against his zipper. "I do," she said, giving him a firm squeeze that had him swearing and slipping off her panties all in the same breath.

# Eight

**M**egan told herself that her constant state of excitement during the following weeks had to do with the secret and highly adventurous nature of their affair. Nick's willingness to indulge her every desire exceeded any expectation she'd ever had about him. Becoming his lover had been the most affirming and uplifting decision of her adult life. It was fast, it was fun. It was exhilarating, it was exhausting. It was all those things and more. But she quickly reminded herself it was anything but love.

On Megan's free afternoons, Nick never seemed to hesitate to leave the construction site early or simply hand off an entire day's work to his second-in-command. On these occasions, she reminded herself that Nick's relaxed attitude toward work had nothing to do with the time they spent together. If he chose to put his job on the line, that was his business. Besides, no matter how exciting their time together was, she was not thinking about giving her heart to the man. The Nick she knew could never be part of the stable future she craved.

Once, when he'd taken off two days in a row, her curiosity got the better of her. She asked him if turning over his responsibilities in such a spur-of-the-moment manner was wise for his career.

"Megan, I took care of everything. Besides, I don't expect to keep this position forever," he said with an amused laugh. "Eventually someone will have to take over the reins."

From that moment on, she decided never to question his availability to her again. There was no good reason to torment herself with the temporary nature of their relationship. The time for him to move on would be here soon enough. Meanwhile, whenever Nick surprised her with plans like a trip to New York City for a carriage ride through Central Park or a day trip through the countryside on the back of his friend's motorcycle, she was ready to share the adventure.

As many times as she was tempted to open up more of her life to Nick, she always remembered the vow she made to herself. Keeping the rest of her life separate was the sanest thing she could do. The sanest thing she *had* to do. Megan looked down at the little girl standing next to her at the school-bus stop and felt her heart grab. Nick was simply passing through her life, she told herself as a lump began forming in her throat, but they were staying here. This was the life she'd chosen, the responsibility she'd taken on, the constant joy she had been blessed with. Through good times and bad, she would always be there for her daughter. Guiding her, protecting her, adoring her. Loving her.

Megan smiled down at her little girl. As hard as she had tried, she hadn't been totally successful in keeping Nick out of Paige's life. Her five-year-old lit up every time she saw the man. Even though Nick had insisted Paige should think the puppy and the doghouse had come from Santa, he'd broken his own rule and presented her with a gift the night before.

"You don't have to keep holding on to it," Megan said, referring to the small gold puppy charm hanging from a chain around Paige's neck. "It won't fall off."

"I'm not holding him, I'm petting him. Nick said I could pretend this is the real Beans. Mommy, isn't Nick wonderful?"

"Yes, Nick's wonderful," Megan said as her thoughts strayed to the times she'd spent with him. What she shared with Nick was an undemanding friendship, incredible sexual chemistry and lots of laughter. That's all she wanted from him, she told herself as she planted a kiss on Paige's head. All she needed from him. All she would ever ask of him. When he moved on, she'd deal with his departure the way she had with every other important passage of their life. Alone.

"I wish Nick was here for when I go on the bus," Paige said as she craned her neck for a look up the street.

Megan made herself smile, even as tears pricked at her eyes. She would make it through a few lonely nights and the inescapable crying jag she knew would come with Nick's inevitable departure, but how Paige was going to react when he left was anyone's guess.

"It's coming!" Paige shouted, pointing to the yellow bus as it rounded the south corner of the town square. She turned her big green panic-stricken eyes toward Megan. "Mommy? I'm scared."

"And pretty excited, too," she said enthusiastically as she took Paige's hand. "Remember? Heather's going to be on the bus. She said she'd save a seat for you. And I'll be here waiting for you when the bus brings you back."

Paige nodded as her gaze roamed nervously up the street, then back to her mother. Megan knelt down on the small patch of grass between the curb and sidewalk. "You're going to have a very exciting day today. Just listen to everything the teacher tells you so when you come back, you can tell me all about kindergarten."

"Okay," Paige said reluctantly.

"And you won't be alone. Remember what Nick said last night?" she asked, pointing to the puppy charm.

Paige swiped at a tear and nodded. "That I'll be the only one who gets to take a puppy to school," she said as her face brightened with a giggly smile.

The next few minutes were a struggle to hold back her own tears as Megan kissed her daughter, then watched her board the bus. As it pulled away, she forced a smile on her face and waved. A full minute after the bus disappeared around the corner Megan made herself turn away.

Her head bowed, she walked back to the door leading into the covered stairway to her apartment. Her *empty* apartment, she thought as she started up the steps. The hollow feeling in her chest took on just enough substance to cause a painful twisting sensation.

It wasn't as if she hadn't seen this day coming for the past five years and knew it wouldn't be an easy one. Maybe planning to take off the entire morning from work was excessive. Then again, the last thing she needed was an audience when she was on the verge of tears, she thought as she made her way slowly up the steps.

Megan grabbed the railing when a pair of leather loafers suddenly came into view near the top. Nick was sitting on the top step, his one elbow planted on his knee and his chin resting in the cup of his hand. He reached to pat the place beside him with his right hand.

She climbed the remaining stairs and took the spot he'd indicated. After a while he spoke.

"Those red shoes she wore are pretty snazzy."

Megan nodded as her pulse pounded in her ears.

He shifted on the step, but kept his eyes fixed ahead of him. "How are you doing?"

"Fine," she said, lacing her shaking fingers around her knees as she managed a one-sided smile. "It's all part of being a single parent. Really. I handle things like this all the time."

He nodded.

She looked away and sighed. "Not fine. I keep seeing crazy pictures in my mind like the school bus being hijacked. Or the teacher taking an instant dislike to Paige. Or worse, Paige will suddenly stop in the middle of finger painting and start screaming for me...and I won't be there," she said before pressing her hand to her lips. Her chin trembled uncontrollably. Her eyes brimmed with tears.

He pulled a handkerchief from his pocket and held it out to her. She took it and began dabbing at her eyes.

"Watching her wave her little hand at me as that bus pulled away..." She gulped back a watery breath as she lowered the handkerchief. "Nick, I've never felt so empty. So..."

Without a word he reached for her. She pressed her face to his chest and sobbed before his arms were fully around her. His steady embrace and soothing presence were a rock she clung to in a sea of floundering emotions. She knew she had no business sharing this weak and needy moment with him, but his comforting presence was too tempting to fight.

He held her five full minutes before she had herself under control again. Pulling back, she wiped the trails of tears from her cheeks. "Sorry. I don't know what got into me. I never get this wacko, but this morning...seeing her off to school for the first time...it really hit me." She rolled her eyes as she gestured with the handkerchief. "Thank heavens I didn't fall apart like this in front of her. I'd never forgive myself." She took a breath and tried for a smile.

"You're a good mother, Megan," he said softly.

She hiccuped once and a new batch of tears started down her cheeks.

"Okay, okay, maybe just average, then."

She looked over the balled handkerchief she held to her nose. Her eyes widened and held before they both began to laugh. After a moment, he shook his head, then looked at his watch.

"Oh, Lord. Look at the time. You're going to be so late for work," she said, checking her own watch as she started to get up. "I'll go get the dog."

He took her hand and urged her to sit. "Actually, I'm catching the hotel's shuttle to Newark Airport in about five minutes. I have a plane to catch."

"A plane?" she asked as his creased khaki trousers and muted madras tie registered with her for the first time. She felt the bottom dropping out of her stomach. Was this it, then? Was this the goodbye she knew would come? "Why?"

"The home office called," he said, reaching for his navy blue blazer hanging on the end of the railing. "They want me to take care of a few problems at a work site out near Reno."

"Nick, are you telling me the truth, or are you in some kind of trouble because of me? Because of the days you've been taking off?"

"Of course not," he said, laughing at her suggestion. "I need to straighten out a few things, that's all. I'll be back in time for Jade's wedding."

"You're going to the wedding?"

"I was surprised myself that I received an invitation. I figure it has something to do with her father being one of River Walk's investors." His smiling gaze turned to a gently probing look. "I hate having to leave you like this."

"I'll be fine. Really, I will. They say the first day of school is harder on the parents." She sniffed. "I've gotten through worse than this."

"I'm sure you have," he said as they stood up. He checked his watch again, then quickly kissed her.

"Rocky Nolan's going to be picking up Beans while I'm away."

Megan nodded. As he started down the steps Megan's newly regained composure began disintegrating. "Nick, wait."

He stopped and turned his head. His steady and patient smile turned her insides to the consistency of whipped marshmallow.

"I…well," she began as she ran her fingers through one side of her hair. "I just wanted to…thank you for coming."

He headed back up the steps and took her in his arms. Before she could think to form a sentence, he leaned her against the wall and kissed her again. Her hungry mouth took everything he had to give. When he finally lifted his lips from hers, he was smiling.

"This is where you're supposed to say you're going to miss me."

She couldn't help herself; she had to say it. "I already do."

He was still laughing as he headed back down the stairs and disappeared out the door at the bottom.

Megan sank down on the top step and leaned her shoulder against the rough shingled wall. She couldn't deny it now, even if she wanted to; Nick Buchanan was the most thoughtful man she'd ever met. He always knew what to say and when to say it, but more important, he knew when to keep silent. And when to back off, too. He could have joined her and Paige at the bus stop, but he chose to allow them that precious moment of passage by themselves. Just as fitting, he was there for her when she needed him most. If she didn't watch herself, she could fall in love with Nick.

Her growing smile froze. Love? Was she losing her mind? She pushed away from the wall and sat up, ramrod straight. How had she allowed such a thought to form?

Shoving up from the step, she turned and started across the porch. This morning's mini nervous breakdown was more serious than she thought. Giving in to her emotions after Paige went had left her vulnerable in places she usually guarded.

She understood fully what she and Nick shared, and while it was ten levels of wonderful, it wasn't love. Love meant commitment, and from the beginning of her relationship with Nick Buchanan she'd willingly accepted that he wasn't the kind of man to stick around for the long run.

She looked at his handkerchief, then stuffed it in her waistband with a shaking hand. A week away from Nick was the best thing that could happen right now. That would give her plenty of time for what she needed most. "A reality check," she mumbled to herself as she briskly rubbed her fingers over a few new tears.

Nick didn't mind the nip in the September night air as he stood outside the screen door of the Chocolate Chip Café's kitchen. All he could think about was how long the eleven days had seemed that he'd spent apart from Megan and how good it was going to be once she turned that always welcoming smile on him. For the first time since he could remember, he felt as if he was coming home. The feeling stemmed from more than the way Follett River had accepted him back after a ten-year absence. Smiling, he leaned his shoulder against the door frame and continued to watch Megan as she worked.

With the steady-handed skill of a brain surgeon, she was carefully attaching a cascade of caramelized stars down the side of a five-tiered cake. Considering her level of concentration, he decided that announcing his arrival right away would be disastrous. Watching her decorating Jade Macleod's wedding cake was a joy in itself. But more than that, he thought with an amused smile, he wasn't quite ready to end his private and highly enjoyable moment of adoration for a woman he'd come to deeply care about.

Several times during his trip he'd come close to phoning her, but he forced himself away from that guarantee of instant gratification. As calculated as he knew it sounded, he'd wanted Megan to miss him. Maybe then, when he returned, she would start sharing a little more of herself with him. Not that she hadn't allowed him occasional glimpses. There had been tender moments in their lovemaking when she would look at him or hold him in a way that made him feel she was a breath away from a breakthrough. At the last second, though, she would draw back to hold her ground in that narrow place in her life that she'd reserved for them.

The only time she'd let her guard down was the morning he'd flown to Reno. Until the moment she'd broken down and sobbed in his arms, he'd tried not to dwell on the way she managed to keep the rest of her life separate from him. But in that sharing moment, he found aching proof in his heart that the bits and pieces weren't good enough anymore.

Starting at the white-blond tresses ribboning from

her slightly askew topknot, his gaze drifted lovingly over her. He smiled to himself as he remembered the sensations those tresses prompted as they touched his body when she made love to him. When she made love to him. God help him, he'd never known such joy.

As she stepped back from the table and absently rubbed her hand against her chin, he pressed closer to the screen and squinted for a better look. Because of her level of concentration, the generous smear of frosting she left below her lips could have been gold dust and she wouldn't have known. He shook his head and smiled when he noticed more creamy smears on one of her eyebrows and both arms and wrists. As the intricate Spanish guitar music playing in the background reached a crescendo, she clamped both hands to her knees to bring herself eye level with the cake. The only thing he found lacking in the sensual tableau she created was eye contact. Of course, once that was established, he wouldn't be satisfied until he was touching her.

She reached to adjust another cascade of caramelized stars and her cropped red sweater slid upward, revealing several tempting inches of skin. He swallowed hard as he remembered her warm, satiny softness and how much he'd been missing it. Adoration was fine to a point, but it did little to stem his need to hold her. The second she began straightening up, he reached for the doorknob.

"Can I get a taste of that?"

Megan closed her eyes, slammed both hands to her collarbone, and whispered in the most exquisitely breathless way he'd ever heard her speak it, "Nick."

"You remembered," he said as she opened her eyes and turned her head fully in his direction.

A smile began forming on her lips as Nick set down his suitcase and locked the door behind him. He turned to face her and the moment began to shimmer with arousing energy. "Ah, Meggie," he teased, "say you *do* remember me. We were lovers once."

"We were?" she asked, fighting a smile as she looked at the frosting clinging to her fingers. Turning her big green eyes to him again, she slipped a finger in her mouth, sucked on it, then slowly pulled it out. The smoldering look that followed was an invitation to continue with the game he'd purposely started. "Why don't you refresh my memory?"

"Okay," he said, loosening his tie and undoing the top button on his shirt. The Spanish guitar music throbbed out a strong and unforgiving beat. "What do you want to know?"

"Were you any good?"

He shrugged. "You never complained," he said, feeling a slow roll of thunder in the lightning-laced heat building between them. He pointed to her fingers. "I'm a starving man. I flew across mountains and deserts just to get back to you. Worse than that, I drove the Jersey turnpike in a rental car. So what do you say?" he asked as she walked over to the center table. He waited and watched as she pushed aside a bowl and lifted herself onto the edge. "Can you spare me a taste of something sweet?" he asked as he walked over to her.

"I'd like to help you out," she said, dragging a thumbnail down her nose to hide her smile. She pointed across the room with her other hand. "But the frosting is for Jade's wedding cake."

He looked over his shoulder at the obviously finished product and the huge chocolate cake sitting farther down the long side table. "I see. But how about this stuff?" he asked, pointing to the frosting on her fingers.

"If you think a little bit of sugar would satisfy—" Her sentence broke off as Nick quickly slid his hands around her waist and lowered his head to a dab of frosting near her navel.

"It's a start," he whispered against the tightening muscles of her abdomen.

She sucked in a breath as he drew his tongue around her navel. After a few well-placed flicks she was wriggling so much that he had to hold her hips steady to finish the job. Long past the time he'd licked her clean, he raised his head and gave her a questioning look. "If you could spare just a little more."

Leaning back, she planted her hands on the table and locked her heavy-lidded stare with his. "Th-that would be fine," she whispered. "Anywhere you want to do that is fine."

"Anywhere?"

Her breathing was visibly escalating along with his. She managed a nod. When he couldn't take his eyes from hers, she whispered, "Whatever you want."

He unbuttoned her sweater, then unhooked the front closure on her bra and pushed the cups aside. The tips of her breasts were already beading with signs of her arousal. The sight of them had his heart pounding through every one of his extremities. He drew his fingers between her breasts, then down to the waistband of her cutoff jeans.

"Why don't you show me what I want."

Although her movements were slow, they were deliberate and unfaltering. She sat up long enough to dip one finger into the bowl. Resting her weight on one hand, she dabbed the creamy mixture on one of her nipples. "Was I right?"

Her blatantly erotic action had him swallowing from a dry mouth. He somehow managed to rasp, "Oh, yes. That's about as right as it gets."

Lowering his head, he gave her nipple and the surrounding area a lavish tongue bath. The sweet taste coupled with the textured tip made his mouth water for more of her. He took a deep breath. If he didn't get control of the situation soon, they'd be making love on the tabletop. A few kisses, some intimate caresses and maybe even a little heavy petting was fine for the kitchen, but he thought about that comfortable, wide bed waiting for them at his suite, or for once, maybe her bed. He lifted his mouth from her breast and smiled.

"So," he said, trying for a normal conversational tone. "What have you been up to since I left?"

"I've been busy and so have you. But I don't want to talk about that now."

"No?"

"Nick, I don't care about where you've been or what you've been doing," she said as she dragged her finger through the bowl of frosting. "I only care that you're here with me now," she whispered as she touched her finger to his lips, then began to lick them.

The feathery sensations of her warm, wet tongue

against his mouth began to replicate themselves on other places of his body. Suddenly, the tabletop wasn't looking so hard after all. He pulled back from her long enough to see that the door leading to the café's dining room was closed.

"Are you sure you want to do this here?"

"Nick," she whispered, grabbing his tie to urge him closer. "I've wanted to do this here for so long it hurts."

"It's a pretty hard table. It could get…a little… uncomfortable," he said as he twisted his neck to take full advantage of the nibbling kisses she was trailing up his neck and over his jawline. He gave in to a shudder from his heightening desire when she began to scrape his earlobe with the edges of her teeth.

"I remember when we were lovers," she said in that voice she'd used during their sexy and nonsensical conversation a few minutes before. "It was you who never complained."

"Then again, if we're careful, maybe it won't have to be too uncomfortable."

"It won't," she said, stopping her tickling kisses long enough to peel off her sweater and bra. "Not if we do it the way I've imagined we would."

Her blatantly sexy look had his libido surging toward the ceiling. "You've really imagined us here?"

"Nick Buchanan," she said, reaching for his tie. "Have you forgotten that I was voted the Girl Most Likely to Surprise Us with Her Secret Fantasies?"

Without another word, he helped her off the table, then began to undress her while she did the same for him. When every article of their clothing was unceremoniously scattered on the floor around them, she brought him back to the edge of the table. "This way," she whispered, twisting herself into his embrace.

# Nine

"Megan, the cake is simply a dream. I'm so happy Jade insisted on those cascading stars instead of flowers," Mrs. Macleod said as she and Rebecca helped the bride-to-be step into her wedding gown. Carefully sliding the ivory sheath up Jade's body, the mother of the bride continued with her praise. "I never doubted you'd create something simply amazing for us, but to think this came out of your café's tiny kitchen…" Mrs. Macleod's voice trailed off as she shook her head in wonder.

"I'm so glad you're pleased, because I enjoyed every minute I worked on it," Megan said as images from the night before appeared in her mind's eye. A slow smile started across her face.

Nick's surprise appearance and their subsequent hour of scaldingly erotic lovemaking had brought back the smile that had been missing from her face since he'd left. Beginning with that first warm kiss to her belly, he'd convinced her that he'd been hungering for her tender touch, her intimate caresses and those magical moments of madness as much as she had been hungering for his. If exhaustion hadn't claimed them, Nick's dwindling supply of condoms from his suitcase soon would have. Even so, they'd still managed to make love on or over every flat surface in the kitchen.

Since he'd effectively and so efficiently made her lonely days without him a thing of the past, she'd been smiling nonstop. The funny thing was, no one questioned her grin. Because of Jade's wedding to Spencer Madison, everyone was smiling today.

"Well, dear, it's just amazing what you managed to create with a little butter cream frosting and a bit of caramelized sugar. Jade and I had tears in our eyes when we saw it."

"She was right," Jade said. "It turned out to be the perfect combination of romance and fantasy."

"Romance and fantasy?" With memories of Nick still fresh in her mind, Megan focused her eyes on the three women. An uneasy smile struggled upward on her face.

"Jade's got something there, Megan," Rebecca said as she worked at fastening the long row of buttons on the beautiful redhead's bridal gown. "You could advertise romance-and-fantasy wedding cakes as your specialty for Piece of Cake."

Megan pressed a hand over the fluttery sensations in her stomach as her high-spirited mood suddenly began to mellow. Why had Rebecca's suggestion struck her so strangely? She ought to be basking in the compliment her friend had just paid to her. Or was there something else that was causing this bewildering re-action? Whatever it might be, this was neither the time nor the place to be thinking about it. Reaching for the organdy bow at the back of Paige's flower-girl dress, she busied herself by retying it.

"Mommy says all those stars are really candy," Paige said. "She says you can eat them."

"Then we'll have to tell the photographer to take plenty of photos," Jade said.

"Why?" Paige asked as she patted the poufed skirt of her flower-girl gown. "Because it's pretty, like my dress is pretty?"

"Because it's pretty, like your dress," Jade said with a nod, "and because once Spencer finds out he can eat them, those stars are going to be nothing but a memory. Of course, that's after he's eaten all those chocolate Smoochies off the top of that yummy-looking groom's cake your mom made, too."

Megan knew she should have been enjoying Paige's childish laughter as it rang through the room, but all she could think about was getting a breath of fresh air and a quiet moment to gather her thoughts. How had this strange mood swing taken such a strong hold on her?

Backing away from the group, she went to the open French doors and stepped out onto the balcony. Music from a string quartet floated through the warm autumn air. Everything was going to return to normal in just a few moments. She wrapped her hands around the wide white railing and let her gaze roam over the guests on the back lawn of the Macleod estate. After all, it was her friend's wedding day. A time for sharing in Jade's happiness. Paige was almost as excited about her role in the day's event as she'd been about receiving her puppy. This was neither the time nor the place to give in to the blue funk barreling down on her.

Halfway into her second deep breath, she spotted a group of men standing outside the huge white lawn tent. She recognized all three of them. There was nothing remotely blue or funky about the handsome men sipping their champagne down there in the shade-dappled afternoon sunshine. One was a happily married man. One was about to become one. And the other...the other was her temporary lover. The object of her manageable madness. Her bad-boy fantasy come true.

Tightening her grip on the railing, she tried telling herself that her relationship with Nick was under control. He was everything she'd asked him to be. Nothing less; nothing more. Even as her mellowing mood began plummeting through the floor, she reminded herself that an occasional moment of self-doubt wasn't unheard of in affairs like theirs. If she could simply shake off this eerie sensation of invisible cobwebs drifting over her, everything would be fine again.

As she continued to watch Nick, she attempted to match his relaxed manner, his spontaneous smiles and the general sense of well-being he seemed to radiate. After a few moments she stopped and hung her head. Marionettes would have done a more convincing job of it than she.

What was happening? Where was that joyful high-spirited air that she'd started the day with? Why couldn't she stay in that place?

She brushed at her forehead as if the desperate gesture could rid her of the weighty reality heading her way. *I just got you back,* she wanted to shout. *What am I doing to myself thinking about the time you'll have to leave?*

"What's happening out there?" Rebecca called out from the bedroom. "Has the governor arrived yet?"

Megan swallowed hard before she turned her face toward her friend who was standing in the doorway. "I don't think she has," she said, keeping a moist but strangling grip on the railing. "I haven't seen any bodyguards."

"Well, anyway, your daughter has a more important question to ask you," Rebecca said as she ushered Paige onto the balcony.

The five-year-old crossed her arms in front of her as she turned up her flower-wreathed head to Megan. "Mommy, why can't I marry Spence, too?"

Megan looked up at the other women. Their wide-eyed exaggerated expressions went a long way in taking her mind off her unsettling thoughts. She leveled a reprimanding stare at the matron of honor. "Rebecca, did you put her up to this?" she asked with a barely contained grin.

Rebecca shrugged. "All I said was that today was so much fun, I thought we ought to have more weddings in this town."

"Mommy, I'm all dressed up!" Paige said impatiently. Grabbing a fistful of her little gown, she lifted the hem to her knees. "Look at my beautiful shoes." Pointing to the pearls sewn to the tops, she continued. "See, they have jewelry on them, Mommy. So, can I marry Spence when Jade does?"

"Sorry, sweetheart, but this is Jade's special day.

You get to be in her wedding, but only she gets to marry Spence.''

"Your mother's right, dear," Mrs. Macleod said as she looked out at the five-year-old and her mother. "But you mustn't look so sad. One day, when you least expect it, you'll find the right man to marry. Someone out there who knows just what to do to make you as happy as Spencer makes Jade." She turned to her own daughter beside her. "Isn't that right, dear?"

"Absolutely, precious," Jade said, her eyes already trained on Paige.

"That's right," Rebecca agreed. "It just takes some of us a little more time than others to find the right one. But when he comes along, you'll know."

"How?"

"Well," said Mrs. Macleod, "one way to know is when he enjoys doing some of the same things as you."

The little girl thought hard for a moment, her green eyes narrowing, her brow furrowing. "You mean, like coloring inside the lines real good?"

As the women enthusiastically agreed, Paige walked across the balcony, wrapped her arms around a baluster and began scanning the guests below.

"I found him!"

"You're kidding," Rebecca said. "It took me ten years to find Raleigh and you found the love of your life in two seconds?"

Paige nodded vigorously. "Yeah, I did."

"Well, let's have a look at him," Rebecca said as she and Mrs. Macleod stepped onto the balcony and headed for the balustrade.

"Is it the ring bearer?" the older woman asked.

"Have you finally decided to forgive Ronnie for tripping you at the rehearsal dinner?"

Megan didn't have to look. She'd known whom Paige was looking for the moment she mentioned coloring inside the lines. And it wasn't the ring bearer.

Paige pointed down to the three hundred guests milling around below. "There he is. See him over there?"

"Tell me who you're pointing to, Paige," Jade said from just inside the bedroom. "I'd come out for a look, but I don't want anyone seeing my gown before the ceremony."

"Nick! I'll marry Nick! He can color inside the lines real good."

"Excellent choice, Paige," Rebecca said as she leveled a look of admonishment toward Megan, "since no one else seems to have snatched him up."

"Yes, Paige, excellent choice," Mrs. Macleod happily agreed as she hugged the little girl. "According to my husband that young man is going places. Nick told him he's in line for a big promotion."

Megan felt her heart stinging in her chest. Those invisible cobwebs were pressing against her body like shrinking leather. "A promotion? Really, Mrs. Macleod? What kind of promotion?"

"I thought for sure you would have heard," the older woman said as she led them all back into the bedroom.

"Why did you think that?" Megan asked as tension pricked like a cake fork between her shoulder blades. Was her carefully tended secret common knowledge? Had Rebecca's wink been more conspiratorial than teasing reprimand? And who else knew?

Mrs. Macleod reached for the train to Jade's gown. "I thought that since you've spent time out at River Walk catering those delicious luncheons my husband keeps raving about, that you'd probably heard Nick talking about his future plans."

"How times have changed," Jade said as she raised her arms to give the women unrestricted access to the sides of her dress. "I can remember when Nick rode his motorcycle across our front lawn. I had all I could do to keep Daddy from calling the police. Now they're doing lunch."

"And he plays basketball at least once a week with my husband, the same man that kept him in detention most of his senior year. Nothing surprises me anymore," Rebecca said as she helped to attach the bead-encrusted train to Jade's elegantly simple sheath. "Honestly, Jade, you look like you could be on the cover of a bridal magazine." She turned her head toward Megan.

"Didn't we always say she was the only girl we knew who could look sophisticated in her gym clothes? And now look at her."

Megan gave Jade a pulse of a smile, then turned to her mother. "Mrs. Macleod?" she asked in as steady a voice as she could muster. "What kind of promotion were you talking about?"

"The Murano Group is probably going to ask Nick to head up their entire West Coast operation," she said, stepping back from Jade. "I'm told that he's been working toward this since the day he started with them. If he accepts—and why wouldn't he?—they'll pull him off the River Walk project and send him out to Los Angeles."

"Raleigh told me that Nick only took this job as a favor to the company, because he's from this area and they thought it would be good for the project. He's worked almost exclusively out West the entire time he's been with the Murano Group."

Megan measured her breaths, if only to keep them coming. Why hadn't she known anything about this? Why hadn't Nick told her? How had this slipped by? She slowly closed her eyes; of course, the answer was so obvious. She didn't know about Nick's future plans because she never wanted to listen to him talk about anything that didn't connect to the immediacy of the moment. "When does he expect to hear?"

All three women looked expectantly toward her as she toyed with her earring.

Jade and Rebecca both spoke at the same instant. "Is this business or personal?" they asked before looking at each other and bursting into laughter.

"Business," she insisted with as much matter-of-factness in her voice as she could manufacture. "I have a catering contract with the Murano Group. Remember?"

"Ah, yes," Mrs. Macleod said. "Those cakes and those wonderful luncheons. Well, the promotion could come through anytime now. Everyone, here and in Los Angeles, is very pleased with the way he's been handling River Walk. All along he's been preparing his men to take over once he leaves. You should ask Nick more about at the reception," Mrs. Macleod said as she turned her attention back to her daughter. "But, right now, I think we all have a wedding to attend."

Fifteen minutes later Megan took her seat in a row of gilded chairs halfway up the aisle. As she waited with the other guests for the wedding to begin, she told herself her moist hands and pounding heart were perfectly normal reactions. At a time like this, didn't every mother of a flower girl experience a little anxiousness? She drew in a shaky breath and turned her attention to Paige. Tears stung her eyes; *this did not,* she reminded herself sharply, *have a thing to do with Nick Buchanan!*

She smiled at Paige as the five-year-old started down the aisle to the strains of the string quartet, several confident steps ahead of the ring bearer. As her daughter dutifully scattered pale yellow rose petals from a satin-lined basket, Megan tried to lose herself in the fairy-tale scene like everyone else.

The tension between her shoulder blades was just starting to become bearable again when Paige's little head snapped to the left, sending her long spiraling curls into a bouncy blond mass beneath the wreath of stephanotis. Her serious expression instantly transformed itself into a beaming smile. Megan's heart lurched against her rib cage; Paige had spotted Nick.

As Paige sent a tiny wave toward the tall, dark and ruggedly handsome man, Megan knew she couldn't pretend anymore. The one thing she'd promised herself she would guard against at all costs had happened. Her daughter had come to adore Nick Buchanan.

And so had Megan.

The next few minutes played out in a teary blur set to one of Bach's *Brandenburg Concertos.* Not that anyone noticed her dabbing at her eyes. Half the women there were in tears. The only difference was, their tears were joyful ones. Megan's were anything but.

By the time Jade and Spencer took their vows, she was certain the lump in her throat was going to choke off her already iffy air supply. It was a miracle that she had enough oxygen going to her brain to form one definitive thought, but against all odds, a few had formed.

She'd made a terrible, selfish mistake.

To continue making it would be worse.

She had to end this thing with Nick.

Today.

Nick hadn't taken his eyes from Megan since the moment she took her seat up the aisle from him. He was mildly surprised that she cried so much during the ceremony. Most of the women there had, too, but there was something about Megan's tears that gave him an odd feeling in his gut. When Paige waved at him, he thought her mother would have shared a smile with him. Instead, she let go of the gilded chair she'd been clutching and pressed her tissue over her eyes with both hands.

Later, at the reception, he watched her for one solid hour as she worked her way around the interior of the tent. She had reminded him the evening before that the rules she'd insisted on at the beginning of their relationship still applied. They weren't going to do anything during the wedding that would start people talking about them. At the time she reminded him, he was nibbling his way up her neck and would have agreed to anything. But before he'd left her at her door, he'd had second thoughts about her insistence that he continue to honor their agreement so stringently, even at a friend's wedding.

"Megan, I can't be in the same place with you for hours and not get to talk to you or touch you at all. I could develop a tic, start salivating," he had teased as he adjusted his khaki trousers, "or something worse."

When she pressed her lips together to keep from laughing, he knew he was making headway. "One dance," he had said, hoping that if he could get her on the dance floor, she'd stay with him for more.

"One," she'd said.

He hadn't expected her to leave a smoking trail to get to him during the reception, but he didn't expect slow motion, either. He'd been patient at first, stealing glances at her as she chatted with people on the opposite side of the tent. While he waited for her to work her way over to his side, he spent the time talking to several investors in River Walk. Two women approached him to confess they'd had big crushes on him during their high-school years.

He checked on Megan's progress several times, convinced she meant to talk with every guest there. Once she had him scratching his head when he lost sight of her for fifteen minutes. If he didn't know better, he'd think she was trying to avoid him. When he finally spotted her alone and partially hidden by a potted palm, he excused himself from his group and went to her.

"One dance," he whispered against the back of her neck when he was sure no one was looking.

Startled, she jerked her half-filled champagne glass as she turned, spilling most of the pale gold liquid onto the grass.

''Nick.'' She stared at him for a long moment, then looked away. ''We have to talk.''

''We can do that while we're dancing.'' He slipped her champagne glass from her hands, set it on a table and offered his hand to her. ''Don't look so nervous. This isn't the senior prom, and though I've looked for them, I haven't spotted a curtain of crepe-paper streamers.'' He took her hand to lead her onto the wooden dance floor, but she dug in her heels and wouldn't budge.

''What's wrong?'' he asked when she wouldn't meet his eyes.

''I should have brought this up last night, but I…we, uh…''

Whatever was upsetting her, he'd expected at least a smile when she mentioned last night. Instead, she flicked a wary gaze his way.

''Are you all right? You're looking a little pale and your hands are freezing. Do you want to sit down?''

She shook her head.

''Do you want to tell me what this is about?''

''While you were away I had a chance to think about things. I realized that I've been letting too many things slide. Now that the wedding's over…'' Her voice trailed off. She rubbed the side of her face and started over. ''Nick, now that the wedding's over, I think it's time for us to…be over, too.''

Nick stared at her profile for a long and disbelieving moment. He stepped closer. ''Over? What the hell are you talking about?''

She looked up at him and was about to speak when one of the waiters passed by on his way out of the tent.

"Look, whatever this is about, we're not going to get it sorted out here. Can you get a sitter for later tonight so we can talk?"

"Talking about this is not going to change anything."

"Megan, for God's sake, tell me what I've done to upset you."

"I'm not upset with you. I'm upset with myself for letting this thing go on so long."

"This thing?"

When she wouldn't or couldn't answer quickly enough for him, he took her hand and pulled her toward the exit. His patience was gone, replaced by a burning need to understand what had happened to make her change so drastically. He didn't stop until he had her on the other side of a privacy hedge that separated a pear orchard from the rolling lawn.

"Start talking."

"Nick, we've had some really wonderful times together. So wonderful that I'm afraid I've been neglecting other parts of my life."

"Has something happened? Megan look at me," he said as he took her downcast face in his hands and turned it up to his. "Did something happen while I was away?"

"Yes. I took a reality check on how my plans for the future were progressing and what I found out was pretty scary. For one thing, I put off writing a check to the rental agency for that house on Kennar Street. The one with two kitchens. Instead, I spent that day with you. The agent told me someone else is interested in it now and I might have to get in a bidding war for it. And two of my waitresses are quitting because their class loads have gotten too heavy. I saw that coming, but I put off doing anything about it. I could give you the long list, but there's only one thing on it that concerns you directly.''

"Tell me and whatever it is, I'll fix it."

"When I saw Paige waving at you as she was coming down the aisle today..." Megan stopped and looked away from him. "It hit me so hard I couldn't breathe. She's crazy about you. Nick, if we let this go on any longer, once you leave, she's never going to trust another man. Not for a long time anyway, and childhood goes by too quickly as it is."

"So your solution is to end it?"

"You know it's the only thing to do."

"Megan—"

"Don't," she said, pressing her hand against his lips.

He took her hand away, but she went on before he could. "Nick, you said the last thing you wanted was to hurt her. Well, stop and think how her face lit up when she saw you there today. How deep are you willing to go into that little heart of hers before you have to tell her goodbye?"

As he took her by the elbows, his pager started in with a loud, intrusive beeping.

"You'd better check it," she said, staring hard at his shoulder. "It could be important."

"It can wait."

"You could be sorry you said that."

He doubted it, but to stop her from going off on this tangent, he decided to check the pager. With an exasperated sigh, he let go of her, stepped back and pushed his suit coat behind one hip. Unclipping the device from his belt, he lifted it closer and depressed a button. His heart, which had been tripping with their conversation, kicked in an extra beat when he recognized the number on the display. Of all times for the home office to page him. He rolled his eyes upward and shook his head. Why now?

"It is important, isn't it?" Lacing her fingers in a tight ball beneath her chin, she gave him a sad smile. "Maybe even news about that promotion."

"How did you hear about that? You never let me get a word in edgewise about my work."

"It doesn't matter how," she said in a whispery voice as she began to back away from him. "Nick, your plans for the future are as important as mine. Go on, you'd better return that call."

"Megan, I've waited this long," he said, taking her by the wrists. "I can wait a few more..." He closed his eyes, clenched his jaw and exhaled slowly. If this was the call he'd been waiting for, there was no more time.

"You can't say you knew this conversation wasn't coming. Sooner or later, one of us had to start it."

"Come here," he said, wanting to take her in his arms and soothe the tension from her body. And maybe from his. Before he had his arms around her, she shoved her hand against the gnarled trunk of a pear tree to prevent him from embracing her. "I just don't see the need to do this right now."

"Well, I see the need for it," she said as she slapped her hand to her breast. Her voice had suddenly gotten higher and tighter. "My plans for the future are on the verge of either coming together for me or falling apart. I've worked too hard to give it all up." She lowered her arm and turned to face him. "If anyone should understand that, you should."

Shoving his hands in his pockets, he stared at the privacy hedge and listened to the laughter and music filtering through from the reception. Everything she said was true, but that didn't help him swallow it any easier. His emotions were taking a twisting, turning ride through a dark house in a surreal carnival, and all he could do was hang on and hope it came to a stop. After a few moments it did. The sounds from the reception sounded miles away. He nodded. "I understand."

"This isn't easy for me, Nick. Please don't think that. What we've shared has been special."

"Special," he repeated tonelessly. He shook his head as that twisting, turning ride hurled forward again. Hell of an exit line. What was she going to say next? *I hope we can be friends?*

"I think we should make a clean break. No muddied sentimental promises about keeping in touch. If you still want catering at the site, I'll send one of my waitresses out with it. And Beans is just about housebroken, so you won't have to bother coming by for him anymore."

He gave a short, gruff laugh. "I've got to hand it to you, Megan. You went into this relationship with the perfect plan. No shared friends to explain this to. Nothing to divvy up. You even get to leave this mess in someone else's garden."

"Don't you dare be cavalier about this," she said, losing her cool for the first time. "If you think this is easy for me, you're kidding yourself. My courage is coming from three glasses of champagne and enough adrenaline to make me fly.''

He knew she was beyond a goodbye kiss, or even a fond embrace. He knew he would be selfishly wrong to ask her for either, but that didn't make the ache to touch her any less painful. Instead, he nodded, a defeated man paralyzed by a truth he'd willingly accepted weeks ago. ''I hear you,'' he said as he stared at the carefully tended shrub.

''I told you, I didn't need forever,'' she whispered before she walked away, leaving him with nothing but his blinking pager, the light scent of vanilla and an emptiness as long and lonely as a blacktop highway in the middle of nowhere.

# Ten

*F*resh from her scented bubble bath, Megan had just slipped into her red silk thigh-high kimono and was pulling it closed when the knock came. A steady, solid, and if she had to describe it further, a strangely familiar knock. Kinking a brow, she quickly tied the sash around her waist and headed for the front of her apartment.

"Who is it?" she called out as she steadied herself against the door and went up on her tiptoes to peer through the peephole. Before she could see out, her heels hit the rug. Her muscles were as soft and shaky as jiggling gelatin from her long soak.

"It's Nick."

Her fingers flattened against the door. Every muscle in her body tightened. The breath she held burned in her chest. Why had he come back? Wasn't it hard *enough these past weeks, trying to put their time to-gether behind her? What reason could he have to be this cruel?*

"Open up, Megan."

"I don't think so."

"We have to talk."

"There's no use talking, Nick. We made our choices. We already said goodbye."

"Open the damn door, or I'll open it," he said, his voice more determined and demanding than she'd ever heard it.

As she released the lock, the last thing on her mind was concern over the gossip his ruckus could cause. It was annoyance, coupled with plain curiosity, that had her jerking open the door.

"Is this really necessary?" she asked, averting her gaze from his as he walked in and closed the door behind him.

"Nothing I've ever done has been more necessary," he said, reaching behind him and twisting the lock into place. "Where's Paige?"

Letting Nick in had been her first mistake. Her second mistake was lifting her head for one look. From the perfectly scandalous fit of his tight jeans and cling-ing T-shirt, he could have been selling them and his attitude from a Times Square billboard.

"She's sleeping over at her friend's." Megan stepped back and wrapped her arms around her waist. "Why do you ask?" she managed to mumble as she locked onto his dark and riveting stare. When he didn't answer, her voice became a whispery sound to her own ears. "Why are you here? Why couldn't you just stay away like we agreed?"

*His answer came without words when he began to smile that smile. The one that was part tease, part challenge and all bad boy. As always, its effect on her was stunning. Shocking. Intoxicating. Her blood was suddenly sizzling through her veins. Her tongue was sticking to the roof of her mouth. She shook her head. How much temptation could she take? "Go away," she said, reaching for the lock.*

*Slamming his hand against the door, he held it closed as he circled her waist with his arm. His deft move managed to slide the loosely tied kimono from her shoulders and send it slipping down her back as he pulled her against his body. The pale swells of her bare breasts were pressing against his black T-shirt, leaving her feeling exposed and vulnerable to his whim.*

*"Megan, listen to me. I'm not going anywhere."*

*"Why? Can't you see you being here is killing me?" she demanded as she struggled to free herself from his irresistible embrace.*

*Ignoring her question, he began to brush his lips slowly yet fiercely over hers. She raised her hands to his chest. She knew she should be pushing him away, but the heat and hardness beneath her fingertips had them lightly dancing across his broad chest. Then, as if her mouth had a will of its own, she began to kiss him back.*

*This was wrong. Sinfully, stupidly wrong. She turned her head from side to side in a halfhearted attempt to escape the pleasures of his touch. Tears stung her eyes. "How many times do I have to say goodbye to you?"*

*"Never again,"* he said as he started to kiss her neck.

*She pulled back to stare at him in disbelief.*

*"It's true,"* he said. *"I'm back for good. You're more important to me than any promotion. I love you, Megan. And I know you love me. So say it. Let me hear you say it."*

*Suddenly, nothing mattered but the truth. The truth she'd kept hidden from herself and from him for so long she thought it might have died. But it was as alive as the heart hammering inside her. "I do love you."*

*As tender as her words were, his next kiss was more so. Then he peeled away the rest of the red silk, and letting it puddle on the floor, he lifted her vanilla-scented body into his arms. The next thing she knew, they were in her room and he was lowering her onto her bed. A second later he was removing his clothes and stretching out beside her.*

*He parted her thighs and as his hot, hard body moved over hers, he gently demanded entrance to the empty place inside her.*

*"Nick,"* she whispered, opening to him as she welcomed him home for the last time.

Turning over in her bed, Megan punched at her pillow, hoping to rid herself of the vivid pictures in her mind's eye. Avoiding Nick was one thing, but how had she deluded herself into thinking that if she worked hard enough she could keep her mind off him? And when was she going to get these fantasies about him under control? There was no place in her life for fantasies or second thoughts and no intelligent reason to entertain them.

Why couldn't she accept their temporary relationship for what it was? A wonderful time that should have become a wonderful memory the moment it ended.

Nick was obviously handling the transition better than her. He'd gone along with her request to make a clean break; she hadn't seen him since the wedding three weeks ago. She couldn't really fault him. He had done everything she'd ever asked him. He'd gone into this relationship knowing its temporary nature. He had even done the gentlemanly thing at the reception by initially resisting the breakup. Then he somehow managed to convince her he wished it could go on longer. At one point, she'd felt herself wavering from her resolve to end it, but when his pager went off it sounded a wake-up call to them both. Their separate futures had waited long enough.

Maybe time would give her back her life. Maybe time would give her strength to resist the urge to stare at the door or listen for the phone. Maybe time would take away the need that stayed with her like a low-grade fever threatening to spike if she lingered over a memory too long.

Time. Days ago there had been too little of it, but try as she did to fill it now, she couldn't. She learned to be grateful for every daily event and minor happening that came her way. From filling last-minute catering requests to volunteering as a parent helper in Paige's kindergarten class, she made certain she was never idle. Still, the days were too long and the nights were filled with fantasies that would never be real. The truth was always one thought away; she'd fallen in love with the man, and it was too late to tell him.

Thank God Paige was handling Nick's absence

from her life better than Megan. For a week after Jade's wedding Megan reminded her five-year-old that Nick wouldn't be by to pick up Beans because the dog was finally housebroken and could stay alone in the apartment. Over the following weeks, Paige asked less and less about Nick. Though her daughter appeared to be doing well, Megan kept a careful watch on her moods. Maybe too careful, she decided after a probing conversation one night late in October.

"Paige, you look sad," Megan said as she reached to hug her daughter.

Paige shook her head, pulled away and reached for her box of crayons. Megan sat down beside her at the coffee table. "That's okay. I understand why you're sad."

The little girl picked out another crayon, fixed it between her fingers and began to tap it like a drumstick on the page she was coloring. Blue dots appeared over the picture. "A million, zillion stars," Paige murmured to herself.

Denial, Megan thought as she picked up a crayon and began coloring the page opposite the one her daughter was working on. The child was involved in some kind of denial, and the best thing she could think to do was get her to talk about it. "You're sad because Nick doesn't come around anymore, aren't you?"

"Mommy—?" Paige began as she tilted her head toward Megan.

"It's okay," Megan said, stroking her daughter's braids. "Nick likes you very much, but you have to understand that he's a busy man. He has lots of work to finish out at River Walk, and then he has a job out in California that's waiting for him. He has plans, just like we do."

Paige made a *tsk*ing sound with her tongue. "I know that."

"You do?"

The little girl emptied the box of crayons onto the table, then picked up a fistful. "You already told me, Mommy. This many times," she said, holding up the crayons to illustrate her point.

Megan sighed and sat back on her ankles. "Then why are you sad?"

"I'm not sad," Paige said as she began lining up the crayons in front of her coloring book.

"And you're not mad at Nick, either?"

"No."

"Then what's wrong?"

"I'm just coloring real careful." Paige moved on her knees closer to Megan and patted her cheeks. "Why are *you* sad, Mommy?"

"Oh, sweetheart," she said, enfolding the little girl in her embrace, "I'm not sad." And for the moment she wasn't sad, because she was convinced her daughter had dealt well with Nick's sudden departure from their lives. "I'm just a little tired," she said before planting a noisy kiss beneath her chin.

Nick stopped pacing inside the trailer long enough to rub the back of his neck and stare at the phone. No. He was not going to call her. Even though he wanted to hear her voice one more time before he flew out to California, it was obvious that Megan didn't share the need. From what he heard she had moved on from that goodbye scene they'd shared during the reception. Her life was on track, her plans humming along.

He knew she was still running the Chocolate Chip Café, and as often as he'd seen her van around town, he knew her catering business was booming. That shouldn't surprise him. Her life was in Follett River. She'd told him often enough, and now she was proving it.

"Good for you, Megan," he mumbled softly to himself as he started pacing again. She was on the brink of getting what she wanted. And so was he. The call he'd been waiting for had finally come through yesterday. The Murano Group had offered him the promotion and wanted him out at the Los Angeles offices by tomorrow noon to talk details.

He walked behind his desk, sat down in his chair with a rushing sigh and rubbed his face. He'd been waiting for years to head up the West Coast operation. So why wasn't he ecstatic, now that it was within his reach? Where was the triumphant surge of adrenaline that he'd expected to keep him wired for a week? Why hadn't he bothered to share the news with his cousin and her family, his employees or his basketball buddies last night? Why had he, instead, only told them half of it—that he was flying out today for a meeting?

He snorted and shook his head. Who was he kidding? He knew the answer to all those questions and more. Megan's absence from his life continued to stay with him like a cold shadow, blocking out any opportunity hinting at happiness. Dammit, he wanted to be angry with her, and in some ways he was. She had decided on the conditions and laid them out to him.

And he had agreed to every one of them. Willingly. Understandingly. Enthusiastically. He had entered into the relationship with his eyes open. Now that they had gone their separate ways, he found himself wondering about the nature of the arrangement. Had he meant little more to her than a fantasy lover come true just long enough to reassure her that she was still desirable?

No one would have faulted him for answering yes to that. Yet something held him back from accepting it as the only explanation. Maybe it was the way she whispered his name over and over when they were finally alone. Maybe it was the way she held him in her arms and kissed him after they'd made love. Or maybe it was that utter vulnerability he saw in her eyes when she thought he wasn't looking. He stared up at the ceiling. Was he kidding himself? Was this inability to simply accept that it was over nothing more than a reaction to his bruised ego? And what was he waiting for? What did he want? A sign that she hadn't transitioned well? To know she doubted her decision to break things off? To find out her bed felt as lonely as his? With a heavy sigh, he looked at his watch, then pushed up from his chair and reached for the tape dispenser. Whatever it was that kept him in this limbo wasn't about to release him anytime soon. In the meantime, this trip to Los Angeles couldn't wait. He slapped the tape to the side of the box and was drawing it across the top when someone knocked on the door, then opened it.

"Boss? You in there?"

"Yeah, Rocky. What's up?" he asked as he ripped off the tape and set the dispenser aside.

"Someone out here wants to see you," he said, gesturing toward the parking lot.

With a weariness that belied his thirty years, Nick slipped on his jacket and followed his second-in-command outside. What he saw made him smile for the first time in days. Neatly assembled beside their school bus was a group of children. Each one was wearing a small yellow safety helmet with River Walk VIP printed on it. He'd known a class from Follett River Elementary School had scheduled a field trip, but he'd left the details to Rocky.

"The short one on the end says she's a friend of yours," Rocky said, pointing to the little blonde who was furiously waving two mittened hands at him.

"Nick! Hi, Nick."

He felt laughter rumbling up from his chest as he crossed the parking lot to where Paige was standing. Or, more to the point, where she was hopping up and down.

"Good morning, Miss Sloan," he said, dropping down to his haunches. He offered his hand to the giggling child. Instead of taking it, she opened her arms and threw herself against him in an over-the-top spirited embrace.

"I miss you, Nick," she said, oblivious to the stares of her classmates and teacher as she rested her cheek on his broad shoulder. "Did you miss me?"

"Hey, I sure did," he said, trying to swallow the prickly ache in his throat as he hugged her back. He carefully cleared his throat as he took her arms from around his neck and stood up. "It's been a long time."

He fixed his gaze on the rest of her classmates and the three adults accompanying them. "Well," he said, raising his voice for everyone to hear, "are you all ready for a VIP tour this morning?"

A loud chorus of affirmatives filled the chilly autumn air.

"That's good. Mr. Nolan is going to take you inside and tell you all about River Walk. He'll be happy to answer all your questions."

The teacher and her aides motioned the line forward. Nick watched as Paige moved across the parking lot. As they stepped onto the boardwalk that ran between the river and the main building, Paige turned. When she saw he wasn't following, she did a dancing skip step back across the parking lot to him.

"Come on, Nick," she said, taking his hand in her mittened one. "Aren't you gonna come with us? We're gonna have pumpkin cupcakes after. My mommy made them."

He looked into her upturned face and those big and trusting green eyes of hers. Eyes so like her mother's it made the ache of losing Megan start all over again. He nodded. "I can spare a few minutes," he said, smiling down at her.

On the way into the atrium a myriad of topics rolled off her tongue. Chattering on excitedly, she caught Nick up on Beans, kindergarten, a rhyme about the alphabet and the red tassels on her boots. Because he was enchanted with her and because he couldn't get a word in edgewise if he had tried, he listened dutifully to all she said, then complimented her on the way she made the tassels move.

"How's your mother?" he finally asked.

Her smiling face softened as she studied Nick for a few moments. "She says we're gonna move to a big house and Beans can peepee in the backyard anytime he wants.''

"She's happy, then?"

"I think so," she said with a shrug. She looked at Nick as her brow wrinkled. "She pretends sometimes."

Nick smiled. "Caught her dancing, did you?"

Paige shook her head. "Not that kind of pretend," she said, pulling off her mittens. They dangled from two yarn strings as she unbuttoned her coat. Nick helped her out of it, then placed it on the growing pile on a nearby table. He motioned to one of the teachers that he was almost done talking with her.

He lowered himself to his haunches again. "What kind of pretend?"

"She pretends she doesn't know Beans sleeps with me. And I pretend that I don't know she sleeps with your picture." Paige wagged a finger at him. "But I know."

"*My* picture?" he asked, touching his fingers to his chest. "Are you sure?"

"Uh-huh. She showed me, when she cut it out of the newspaper. You had this kind a hat on you," she said, touching the brim.

Nick nodded as his pulse began pounding in his throat. The photo had appeared in the *Follett River Ledger* three weeks earlier as part of a photo essay about River Walk. "Does she do that every night?"

Paige nodded. "Every night." Her smile faded again as she leaned close to his ear. "Sometimes she cries. I pretend I don't hear her, but I do," she whispered.

"Why do you think she cries?"

"I don't know," she said, shrugging again. "She says she's not mad at Beans because he peed on the rug two times." Paige's face suddenly brightened. "She used to laugh more when you used to come to see us. You should come see us today, Nick."

"I can't make it today," he said, his mind still racing with the news that *Megan slept with his picture.* All these weeks when he thought she'd put their time behind her so easily, she'd been crying herself to sleep about him. He didn't know whether to laugh out loud or kick himself on the backside for feeling so damned happy about this news.

"I know. You can't come because you're busy," Paige said, her little voice weighty with undisguised disappointment.

"Yes," he said, lifting her hands to give them a peppering of tiny kisses that made her laugh. "I have to fly to California today."

"Mommy told me you were gonna go there. Will you ever come back, Nick?"

He nodded. "Sure, I will," he said, leading her over to join her group by the colorful display map. He started to leave, but she grabbed his arm.

"Promise?"

"I promise."

# Eleven

Rebecca laced her fingers together in a prayerlike attitude, leaned over the counter at the Chocolate Chip Café and frowned with more seeming discomfort than Megan had ever seen.

"Please, Megan," she begged, while the bell over the front door was still jangling. "I know it's last minute and you have a million things to do. And you know I wouldn't ask you if it wasn't a matter of life or death—"

"This is all my fault, really," Jade cut in, leaning her elbows on the counter next to Rebecca's and patting Megan's hand. "Spence and I got back from Paris yesterday and Raleigh and Rebecca met us at the plane. We insisted they go out to dinner with us in New York and time just slipped away. It was too late to call you by the time we got into Follett River last night."

"Call me about what?" Megan asked, halfway laughing at her two friends who had just rushed in from the cold autumn afternoon. "I'm getting another gray hair standing here listening to this buildup, so if you two could fast-forward to the good stuff..."

"I need a cake for tonight," Rebecca said.

"Tonight?" Megan looked at her watch and then the clock on the wall. "Oh," she said, shaking her head. "I don't think there's enough—"

"Please, don't say that."

"What's going on?"

"You know the ribbon-cutting ceremony for River Walk is scheduled for tomorrow. There will be a ton of people all over the place out there."

Megan made a production of wiping her already clean hands on a tea towel. She didn't care about the ton of people, just one man. The buzz around the café all week long had been that Nick Buchanan was coming back to Follett River just for the ribbon cutting.

"You're going tomorrow, aren't you?" Jade asked.

"No. I have a catering job in the afternoon and I'll be too busy." An insane part of her brain wanted one last look at him before he flew off to the West Coast for good, but the rest of it was more interested in survival. If she didn't have that catering job, she'd spend the time cleaning out her closets. Or knitting a sweater for Beans! Anything but go to that ceremony.

"Don't worry about not going, Meggie. We'll tell you all about it," Rebecca said, "but in the meantime, I have this problem. I invited my staff over to my new offices at River Walk for a private little launch party. Tonight. Megan, please say you'll come through for me and I'll owe you for the rest of my life."

"It's four o'clock. I don't see how I could possibly get all my work done here and bake a cake. And I have to pick up Paige at Aunt Sandra's in twenty minutes."

Rebecca and Jade looked at each other. "No problem," they chorused.

Rebecca pushed off the counter and headed behind it. "I'll take care of the café while you get started on the cake. You know I'm a whiz with that thing," she said, pointing to the cappuccino machine.

"And I'll pick up Paige. Spence and I brought her a little present back from Paris. Would it be all right if I take her out to my parents' for dinner with us?" Jade asked, backing away from the counter on the way to the door.

Megan shrugged and opened her palms. "Okay. That's really nice of you. I'll just go in the back and telephone Aunt Sandra that you're coming." She looked at Rebecca and smiled. "What kind of cake?"

Rebecca let out a loud and dramatic sigh. "You're an angel! Mocha nut with fudge frosting. Heavy on the fudge."

Megan felt her smile disappearing. She hadn't made mocha nut cake with fudge frosting since she and Nick went their separate ways. It was Nick's favorite cake. She nodded quickly, refusing to slip into a depression over that fact. "What time will you be by for it?"

"Well, that's another thing. I have to be out there in two hours to set up. Oh, and Raleigh's teaching a class until nine. Could you bring it out at eight? Please. Pretty please."

Megan rolled her eyes as she walked by her friend and into the kitchen. "As if you'd take no for an answer."

At five minutes to eight that evening, Megan walked across River Walk's parking lot, trying her best not to stare at the new bank of junipers at the east end. The space had once been home to the construction-site trailer. By the time she pushed open one of the glass doors and walked into the atrium area, she'd successfully gotten her mind off the trailer. She was now thinking about Nick and how he'd looked that day up on the roof. This time she made a point of not crushing the cake box in her hands. Instead, she smiled at a few people she knew who were checking on last-minute details for tomorrow's ceremony.

As soon as she handed the cake over to Rebecca, she was leaving. The last thing she wanted to do was run into Nick if he was anywhere nearby. Hurrying up the steps, she moved quickly over to the office marked New Horizon. The blinds were closed on both the door and the window, but the lights were on inside.

"Rebecca," she called out as she pushed the partially opened door and stepped inside.

No answer.

She placed the cake box on the desk nearest the door, shrugged out of her coat and went to look in the back rooms for her friend. Megan frowned. No Rebecca and no sign of any party preparations. What was going on? she asked herself as she stepped back into the front office. It was then she noticed a note taped to the screen of one computer. Bracing her hands on the desk, she leaned in to read the note: *!!! DON'T LEAVE !!!*

"Six exclamation points," she mumbled, arching a brow. That was a lot even for Rebecca. Tapping her nails on the desk, she glanced at her watch. "I'll give you six minutes, girlfriend, and then I'm leaving."

"How about me? Will you give me six minutes?"

Her heart was in her throat before her head snapped upward. "Nick," she whispered, staring at him in the doorway. She pushed up slowly from the desk. "I didn't know—"

"You didn't know I'd be here."

She nodded as she rubbed her hands together and looked away. Not that that did much good. She could feel his presence in every part of her body. She could taste him on her mouth.

"I was just dropping off a cake for Rebecca." From the corner of her eye she could see him nod. This was the time to tell him she had to leave. This was the moment she should be heading for the door. Instead, she picked at the string tied around the cake box.

"How's Paige?"

"Oh, you know Paige. Unstoppable." She shook her head and tried for a smile, but the weight of what she'd been missing made it impossible. "I, uh, hear you got the promotion. Congratulations," she said, lifting her gaze to him. He nodded. Now all she had to do was remember how to breathe and she might get out alive.

"I heard you rented the house over on Kennar."

She nodded.

"You don't look very happy about it."

"Sometimes I think I am." Shaking her head, she waved her hands as if to wipe away what she'd just said. Her words and gestures had as much grace as boxcars bumping together. "I mean, of course I am. We're moving over there in a few weeks. Paige is sure that's going to be as much fun as Christmas morning. Kids," she said, fiddling with her cuffs, then smoothing her fingers over her belt buckle. "They're so...funny."

Nick tested the edges of his teeth with the tip of his tongue. Her hands were shaking. So were his. It was time to make his move. Walking over to where she stood, he tapped his finger on the cake box. "May I have a look?"

"Sure."

She reached to untie the string at the same moment as he did. His fingers fumbled with hers, but instead of pulling back from him she froze. He drew his hand across hers.

"Megan—"

"Nick, don't."

"Don't what?"

She looked up at him through teary eyes. "Don't make me fall in love with you all over again."

He smiled. It had to be one of the more peculiar ways to declare love, but he wasn't complaining. He drew his hand up her arm and turned her around to face him. "I wouldn't dream of it. You're quite capable of doing that all by yourself. You've just had a hell of a time admitting it. Even to yourself."

"Why did I say that to you?" she whispered, pressing her hand to her forehead. "I'm sorry. This is all so crazy. I swore if I saw you, I wasn't going to do this."

"Why is it crazy?" he asked quietly as he warmed her cold hands in his. He'd never felt saner in his life.

"Because I can't keep saying goodbye to you."

"You won't have to ever again."

"Don't you think I know that?"

He shook his head.

"What? Why are you doing that?"

"We really have to make a point of working on our communication skills. Don't get me wrong, sweet girl," he said, wiping a tear from her chin. "We've managed to communicate a whole range of interesting ideas to each other. But we have to work at making sure we're being absolutely clear when we're saying things to each other like, 'I love you' and 'I turned down the promotion' and 'Megan, your mouth is open.'"

"'I love you?'" she finally managed.

"That's right," he said, enjoying the soft look in her eyes as he nodded. Suddenly, her eyes grew wide.

"You turned down the promotion?"

"That'll take a little longer to explain, but since I'm moving to Follett River I'll have the time. Just trust me, Megan, it was the right thing to do. Now, about that mouth of yours…"

She opened it in a teasing gasp.

"Well," he said, cupping her face in his hands, "if you're not going to close it…" He leaned down and kissed her. When he stopped a full minute later, it was to ask her to marry him.

"Let me make this perfectly clear," she said, laughing and crying at the same time. "Yes. There. How did I do?"

He started to smile. "That was a great start."

# Epilogue

——

"So, you're really going to sell the café?" Jade asked as Megan placed a caffe latte on the table in front of her.

"That's right," Megan said. "The Chocolate Chip Café is about to become history. It's also about to become a vegetarian restaurant."

"I'm going to miss this place," Rebecca said as she stirred sugar into her own caffe latte. "The first time I kissed Raleigh in public was right over there." She pointed to the window seat. "Remember, Megan?"

"I'll never forget it. You were stenciling reindeer on the window for me when he came in. The next thing I knew, you'd grabbed his tie and pulled him down for a kiss."

"I wish I'd seen that," Jade said as Megan and Rebecca laughed. "But I have a few memories, too.

This was the first public place I ever took Spencer. Remember, I was trying to keep him under wraps? As if that were possible!''

Both Megan and Rebecca nodded.

''Even though I told him not to say it, he kept telling people he was my *personal* assistant. So I sent him over to the pharmacy to buy a box of tampons. He never even flinched. He just went out and bought them,'' she said before bursting into laughter with her friends.

As they dried their eyes with paper napkins, Megan realized the two women were looking at her now. Waiting.

''There's nothing to tell. Hey, let's talk about a Christmas wedding.''

''Hold that wedding talk, girlfriend. I want to hear a story first,'' Rebecca said. ''Meggie, your face is ten shades of shameless.''

''Why not? She was voted the Girl Most Likely to Surprise Us with Her Secret Fantasies.'' Jade tucked her red hair behind one ear and gave Megan a tantalizing wink. ''So tell us, Megan, was Nick surprised with your secret fantasies?''

''Very,'' Megan said, then made a zipping motion across her lips. ''Listen, before the guys get back from their basketball game, I have to know something. When did you catch on to Nick and me?''

''Remember that first night he came to see you here at the café? We had met on the street a little while before that and he asked about you.'' Rebecca made a quick, flat gesture with her hand. ''I swear, I knew he was interested in you before he did.''

''What about you, Jade?''

"It took me a little longer. When you showed up at my bridal shower without my gift and turned four shades of pink, I just knew there had to be a man on your mind. So I talked to Reb after the shower and she was happy to share what she knew. She also told me she was pretty sure you were keeping quiet about it."

"So why *did* you keep it secret? From us, I mean," Rebecca said.

"Honestly?" Megan looked across the empty café as snow drifted down outside the windows. "The men you two fell in love with weren't going away. Nick was. As long as it was just the two of us, I could pretend he was staying. But if I told you, then every time I saw you with Raleigh or you with Spence, I'd have been reminded just how temporary my time with Nick was."

The women sat in silence for a few seconds. Then Rebecca spoke. "It's all worked out so well. Although I thought I'd never get you to agree to bake that cake and take it out to River Walk."

"Thank heavens the Murano Group decided they couldn't do without Nick," Jade said. "I think it's wonderful that they gave him the East Coast operation, and that he gets to run it out of office space at River Walk."

"You know what I think?" Megan asked as the café door opened and their men walked in. "I think we should have been voted the Girls Most Likely to Live Happily Ever After."

\* \* \* \* \*

**SILHOUETTE**

*Desire*

# COMING NEXT MONTH

## THE COWBOY STEALS A LADY  Anne McAllister

*Man of the Month*

Shane Nichols intends to kidnap his best friend's girl to stop her marrying another man. Only he steals the wrong woman! Good thing too, as when they get snowbound they have to do *something* to keep warm...

## BRIDE OF THE BAD BOY  Elizabeth Bevarly

*Comet Fever*

Clearly the myths about a matchmaking comet passing over town *must* be true. How else can Angie Ellison explain her shotgun marriage! And the fact that she can't wait for her wedding night...

## THE EDUCATION OF JAKE FLYNN  Leandra Logan

Jake Flynn thinks he understands women. But when his presents for two sisters are mixed up, 'sensible' schoolteacher Nadine gets the piece of sexy lingerie! And Jake finds he has a lot to learn...

## HER TORRID TEMPORARY MARRIAGE
### Sara Orwig

Josh Brand is looking for a nanny but all he keeps getting are husband-hunters! So he strikes a deal with his neighbour Mattie Ryan. He knows they can keep things business-like—if only he can keep his eyes off those long, sexy legs of hers...

## THE KIDNAPPED BRIDE  Metsy Hingle

*Right Bride, Wrong Groom*

Slung over the broad shoulders of her ex was *not* how Lorelei Mason had planned to spend her wedding day. Jack Storm left her at the altar once; now he has the nerve to want her back!

## THREE-ALARM LOVE  Carole Buck

Fire-fighter Keezia Carew never imagined that her best friend's kisses would send shivers up her spine...or that sexy Ralph Randall would propose! At first she turns him down, then she changes her mind and then *he* isn't sure! Will they ever make it down the aisle?

# COMING NEXT MONTH FROM

**SILHOUETTE**®

## Sensation
*A thrilling mix of passion, adventure and drama*

**CAPTIVE STAR** Nora Roberts
**A MARRIAGE-MINDED MAN** Linda Turner
**BRANDON'S BRIDE** Alicia Scott
**KNIGHT ERRANT** Marilyn Pappano

## Intrigue
*Danger, deception and desire*

**HER HERO** Aimée Thurlo
**FORGET ME NOT** Cassie Miles
**FLASHBACK** Terri Herrington
**HEART OF THE NIGHT** Gayle Wilson

## Special Edition
*Satisfying romances packed with emotion*

**TENDERLY** Cheryl Reavis
**FINALLY A BRIDE** Sherryl Woods
**THE RANCH STUD** Cathy Gillen Thacker
**LITTLE BOY BLUE** Suzannah Davis
**DADDY'S HOME** Pat Warren
**HER CHILD'S FATHER** Christine Flynn

# CHRISTIANE HEGGAN

## SUSPICION

Kate Logan's gut instincts told her that neither of her
clients was guilty of murder, and homicide detective
Mitch Calhoon wanted to help her prove it. What neither suspected was how dangerous the truth would be.

*"Christiane Heggan delivers a tale that will leave you
breathless."*

—Literary Times

1-55166-305-8
**AVAILABLE IN PAPERBACK
FROM SEPTEMBER, 1998**

# 4 FREE
## books and a surprise gift!

We would like to take this opportunity to thank you for reading this Silhouette® book by offering you the chance to take FOUR more specially selected titles from the Desire™ series absolutely FREE! We're also making this offer to introduce you to the benefits of the Reader Service™—

- ★ FREE home delivery
- ★ FREE gifts and competitions
- ★ FREE monthly newsletter
- ★ Books available before they're in the shops
- ★ Exclusive Reader Service discounts

Accepting these FREE books and gift places you under no obligation to buy; you may cancel at any time, even after receiving your free shipment. Simply complete your details below and return the entire page to the address below. *You don't even need a stamp!*

**YES!** Please send me 4 free Desire books and a surprise gift. I understand that unless you hear from me, I will receive 6 superb new titles every month for just £2.50 each, postage and packing free. I am under no obligation to purchase any books and may cancel my subscription at any time. The free books and gift will be mine to keep in any case.

D8YE

Ms/Mrs/Miss/Mr..................................Initials ...............................
                                                                          BLOCK CAPITALS PLEASE
Surname ....................................................................................................
Address ....................................................................................................

....................................................................................................

....................................................Postcode................................

**Send this whole page to:**
THE READER SERVICE, FREEPOST, CROYDON, CR9 3WZ
(Eire readers please send coupon to: P.O. BOX 4546, DUBLIN 24.)

# Jayne Ann Krentz

## A Woman's Touch

He was her boss—and her lover!
Life had turned complicated for Rebecca Wade when she
met Kyle Stockbridge. He *almost* had her believing he
loved her, until she realised she was in possession
of something he wanted.

*"...one of the hottest writers in romance today."*

—USA Today